"You must b   get to the point."

Finally.

"I know we were supposed to forget all about what we did together the last time we saw each other, and believe me, I was fully on board with that. In fact, given the way you stalked off and left me there, I would have been perfectly happy never to lay eyes on you ever again. As an exit strategy, yours leaves a lot to be desired. But unfortunately, keeping out of each other's way is no longer possible."

"Why not?"

"Because that night created a situation."

"What sort of a situation?"

She pulled her shoulders back and looked him straight in the eye. "I'm pregnant, Alex," she said. "And the baby's yours."

Lucy King spent her adolescence lost in the glamorous and exciting world of Harlequin when she really ought to have been paying attention to her teachers. But as she couldn't live in a dreamworld forever, she eventually acquired a degree in languages and an eclectic collection of jobs. After a decade in southwest Spain, Lucy now lives with her young family in Wiltshire, England. When not writing or trying to think up new and innovative things to do with mince, she spends her time reading, failing to finish cryptic crosswords and dreaming of the golden beaches of Andalucia.

Books by Lucy King

Harlequin Presents

Stranded with My Forbidden Billionaire

Passion in Paradise

A Scandal Made in London

Lost Sons of Argentina

The Secrets She Must Tell
Invitation from the Venetian Billionaire
The Billionaire without Rules

Passionately Ever After...

Undone by Her Ultra-Rich Boss

Heirs to a Greek Empire

Virgin's Night with the Greek
A Christmas Consequence for the Greek
The Flaw in His Rio Revenge

Billion-Dollar Bet

Boss with Benefits

Visit the Author Profile page
at Harlequin.com for more titles.

EXPECTING THE GREEK'S HEIR

LUCY KING

PRESENTS

Harlequin®
PRESENTS™

ISBN-13: 978-1-335-93970-8

Expecting the Greek's Heir

Recycling programs for this product may not exist in your area.

Harlequin Enterprises ULC
22 Adelaide St. West, 41st Floor
Toronto, Ontario M5H 4E3, Canada
www.Harlequin.com

Printed in Lithuania

MIX
Paper | Supporting responsible forestry
FSC® C021394
www.fsc.org

EXPECTING THE GREEK'S HEIR

CHAPTER ONE

THE GLOBAL ECONOMIC FORUM—taking place in a seven-star resort in Switzerland, with the world's most influential movers and shakers from business, the arts, government and science in attendance—had been running for three days.

That afternoon, Alexandros Andino had given a keynote speech to a packed-out auditorium about future trends in climate change investment. Tonight, at this drinks party, the last social event before everyone departed tomorrow afternoon, he was nursing a glass of whisky surrounded by half a dozen people who sought his further insight on the subject.

Up until a moment ago, he'd had plenty. When it came to alternative energies, green initiatives or the rapidly improving rate of return in this sector, there was little he didn't know.

Right now, however, he had none.

He had nothing to say about anything, in fact.

Because he'd just spotted Olympia Stanhope chatting up playboy businessman Sheikh Abdul Karim al-Umani—his most important, most lucrative client—and through the red mist suddenly swirling about his head like a tornado, all he could think was, that was it. His patience was at an end. He'd finally had enough.

When she first burst onto the investment-fund scene as the director of new business for Stanhope's, the exclusive private bank owned by her super-wealthy Anglo-Greek family, he hadn't thought much of it. Who would ever take seriously a notorious wild child with a decade in the gossip columns and a twelve-week spell in rehab under her belt? he'd privately scoffed when he'd learned of her absurd appointment in November last year. She had no experience of financial markets. According to the tabloids that recorded her every move, all she knew about money was how to spend it. No one would pay her a blind bit of notice. She was simply being indulged by her older brother Zander, who ran the Stanhope Kallis banking and shipping empire, and evidently had no problem with nepotism. She'd be replaced within a week.

In retrospect, that arrogant disregard for her talents had turned out to be a mistake. He'd been an idiot to assume that a too-rich, over-indulged party girl was all she was. He'd underestimated the power of her scandalous appeal to the ultra-high-net-worth individuals that his and others' funds served. He'd failed to consider her uncanny ability to sift the wheat from the chaff, to lure the former to her team and subtly discard the latter. Instead of slinking ignominiously from the financial pages back to the gossip columns where she belonged, she was being tipped as someone to watch. A potential key player in the field that she'd entered with zero previous experience and occupied for a mere six months.

Frankly, it beggared belief.

But because the investors she'd won over to date were relatively small fry, and he remained convinced she was a flash in the pan that everyone would soon see through, Alex had contained his irritation. Because he was no more immune to her charms than anyone else—despite the fact that she descended from a woman he hated with a passion, which should have turned him right off, but for some unfathomable and frustrating reason didn't— he'd given her such a wide berth that they'd barely ever spoken.

However, tonight, by audaciously targeting the multi-billionaire Sheikh whose money he managed, she'd overplayed her hand.

This was *his* world, he thought, gritting his teeth as the sound of her low throaty laugh reached his ears and triggered an unwelcome rash of goosebumps prickling every inch of his skin. A world he'd had no choice but to step into in the aftermath of her mother's affair with his father two decades ago, which had led not only to the destruction of his family and the brutal yet necessary severing of all ties with her son Leo—Olympia's eldest brother and his then best friend—but also, thanks to an extremely acrimonious and expensive divorce, the threat of penury.

He'd spent twenty years sweating blood to turn the ashes of the Andino fortune into an empire that managed so many billions of dollars it was too big to ever be wiped out again. Olympia was trying to muscle her way into the industry he dominated on the back of little more than her family name. Her frothy presence in his space and the undeserved interest she generated was an insult to all his hard work. He could not allow it to continue. She needed to be put in her place before she became all anyone talked about, and what was left of his peace of mind vanished.

With his pulse thudding in his ears and a burning sensation tightening his chest, Alex gave a curt nod and a terse smile as he muttered his excuses to those around him. Then, with a set of his jaw and a sharp surge of adrenaline, he set off in her direction.

She stood with her back to him. Her long dark hair shone beneath the soft light of the chandeliers. Her outrageously flashy silver-sequin dress clung to her curves and shimmered like a beacon in a sea of grey, navy and black. Always standing out, he thought grimly as he cut a swathe through the throng, his eyes narrowing at the sight of the Sheikh touching her on the arm. Always the centre of attention. Like mother, like daughter—dangerous, unpredictable and in possession of the potential to unleash devastation.

Steeling himself not to respond to the impact of her proximity, which he knew from the one and only time he'd experienced it was as intense as it was unwelcome, he came to an abrupt stop beside them.

'Good evening, Abdul Karim,' he said, ignoring her completely as he leaned forward to clap the other man on the shoulder in a move designed to demonstrate his authority. 'Good to see you. Forgive me for interrupting, but would you excuse us? Miss Stanhope and I need to have a word.'

'Right this minute?' The Sheikh's eyebrows rose in a way that suggested he was not best pleased at the intrusion, but those choppy waters would have to be soothed another time.

'I'm afraid it can't wait.'

Abdul Karim eyeballed him for a moment. Then, evidently noting the hint of steel in Alex's tone that belied his relaxed stance and easy smile, he inclined his head and took a step back. 'In that case, of course.'

'Mr Andino is mistaken,' Olympia cut in smoothly, addressing the Sheikh with an effortless smile of her own. 'We do not have and never have had anything to discuss. We haven't even met. Not properly, at least. I can't imagine what words he thinks we need to exchange.'

'I beg to differ,' he countered. 'It's a matter of some importance.'

'I have a gap in my schedule tomorrow morning at nine,' she said, flicking him a glance so chilly it could have frozen the Sahara. 'I could fit you in then.'

'Not tomorrow. Now.'

'Now is not convenient.'

'The urgency of the situation dictates otherwise.'

'Perhaps you could elaborate?'

'I will. In private.'

'As fascinating as this dynamic is,' said the Sheikh, clearly bored of the polite but thinly veiled battle for control playing out before him, 'it's getting late, and I should be heading off. I would, however, be interested to hear more of your thoughts about the future of fossil fuels, Alex. Lunch next week, perhaps?'

'I'll set it up.'

'It was delightful to meet you, Miss Stanhope. I do hope we cross paths again.'

'You can count on it.'

'Good evening.'

With a nod and a smile at each of them in turn, Abdul Karim walked off. Vowing that his client and Olympia would never meet again if he had any say in the matter, Alex clamped a hand to her elbow and wheeled her away before she could escape.

'Let me go this minute,' she hissed, instantly

losing the dazzling smile as she tried but failed to shake him off. 'What the hell do you think you're doing?'

Steering her towards the exit while ignoring the curious looks darting in their direction, Alex gritted his teeth and focused. Despite having braced his defences to withstand her effect on him, her captivating scent nevertheless ignited his nerve-endings. Awareness sizzled through him. The palm that was in contact with her arm felt as though it was on fire and his pulse raced. All of which was frustrating and unacceptable and meant that he needed to get this over and done with as quickly and efficiently as possible.

'I could ask you the same thing.'

'*I'm* not the one causing a scene. How dare you take advantage of your superior physical strength to maul me about as if I'm some sort of chattel? What's going on? Please remove your hand from my arm at once.'

'In a moment.'

'This is outrageous.'

Ignoring her ire, Alex hustled her out of the ballroom. On spying a fire exit, he marched her across the sumptuously carpeted floor, through the door and into the dimly lit stairwell, which would afford them the privacy this conversation required. The second the door swung closed behind them, he released her and shoved his hands into the pockets of his trousers.

Olympia sprang back and rubbed her elbow, her glare so fierce it could have stripped the paint from the ceiling. 'You made me look like an idiot back there, you patronising, misogynistic jerk,' she fumed quietly, her colour high, her dark eyes sparking with simmering fury. 'It was mortifying and utterly out of order. You've done your very best to avoid me for months, and *now* we suddenly need a word? At a drinks party? When we've been here for three days already and I'm right in the middle of something? What's so urgent?'

Alex's stomach churned. His muscles clenched. Keeping a lid on the heat raging through him, and resisting the urge to lower his gaze to the rapid rise and fall of her chest, was taking every drop of will-power he possessed. 'Stay away from my clients, Olympia.'

Her eyebrows shot up and her jaw dropped. 'I *beg* your pardon?'

'You heard,' he said flatly. 'You've been trespassing on my territory for months now and I've let it slide. The low-hanging fruit you've been picking off to date is of little importance to me. But tonight, by approaching Abdul Karim, you crossed a line. You've overstepped and I won't tolerate it any more. So it stops. All of it. Now.'

For a moment she just stared at him. Then twin

spots of colour hit her cheeks. '*Your* territory?' she echoed with a mutinous jut of her chin. 'You *let it slide*? Your arrogance is truly breathtaking.'

So what if it was? As if he'd ever cared about that. 'This is my world, not yours,' he ground out. 'I've been at it for twenty years. I'm the best in the business, the biggest shark in the sea. You are a minnow, splashing around in the shallows. An inexperienced upstart who's waltzed into my industry on her name and nothing else and has ideas way above her station.'

'Yet you evidently see me as a threat,' she shot back, irritatingly uncowed.

'Don't be ridiculous.'

'And you know what? You're right to be concerned about the Sheikh. Because I can be very persuasive when I put my mind to it.'

He could imagine. How many men had she slayed with those dark come-to-bed eyes and the charm that she wielded like a weapon? How many more did she have lined up? Why was he suddenly grinding his teeth?

'The Sheikh is and always will be mine,' he said, unclenching his jaw, scrubbing all thoughts of kissing her from his head and focusing on the point. 'Far more experienced operators than you have tried to lure him away from my company and failed. You're wasting your time.'

'Am I?'

'Your mule-headed naiveté demonstrates how totally out of your depth you are.'

'That's rude.' She took a step towards him and he resisted the urge to retreat. 'But you can think what you like. I may not have been at this for long, and I know I have much to learn, but I have no intention of stopping. In fact, I've barely even begun. There are no lengths to which I won't go to squeeze every drop of success from the opportunity I've been given. I have big plans. *Huge* plans. So I hope you can handle a little healthy competition.'

Refusing to recognise elements of his youthful self in what she said, because identifying with her in any way was the very *last* thing this situation required, Alex inhaled deeply and fought for calm. 'Do not make an enemy of me, Olympia.'

'Or what?'

'You'll regret it if you do.'

'These feel like empty threats,' she said with a dismissive shrug that only intensified the red mist in his head.

'They're anything but. Have you heard of Naxos Capital Assets?'

'No.'

'Lincoln Masters?'

'No.'

'Precisely. Mess with me at your peril. Stay in your lane and out of my business or suffer the consequences. Continue to defy me and I will use any weapon at my disposal to get what I want—your past, your family, every single thing I can find out about you. It will all be fair game.'

'I doubt you'd find anything that isn't already in the public domain.'

'I won't warn you again.'

'And *I* won't be intimidated.' She planted her hands on her hips, the glint of challenge lighting the dark depths of her eyes. 'What exactly is your problem with me, Alex?' she asked as a fire began to burn in the pit of his stomach. 'And don't try and claim that what's going on here isn't personal. We both know it absolutely is. You can't stand me, can you? That much became clear when I tried to introduce myself to you at that awards ceremony back in November. I mean, there I was, holding out my hand for you to shake, and you just looked down your nose at me, then spun on your heel and walked away. It was quite the snub. I don't think I'll ever forget it. Your dislike of me has been apparent ever since. Whenever we find ourselves in each other's vicinity, you avoid me. You glower at me from afar. If looks could kill I'd be dead a thousand times over and I just don't get it. You and I don't know each other. Before tonight we hadn't even spoken. So have I wronged you somehow? Do you take issue with my reputation? I once overheard you commenting that I ought to find a different career to play at, but surely you can't have *that* big a chip on your shoulder. As you pointed out, you're the best in the business and have been for years. If you want the truth, your precious Sheikh was more interested in getting me to agree to dinner than moving his assets to Stanhope's, and believe me I tried. So why do you care what I do? Why do I even show up on your radar? What have I done to make you hate me so much?'

She stopped, her eyebrows raised, her chin up, tension and defiance radiating from her every pore. Alex reeled, buffeted by her accusations and flummoxed by her questions.

So much for assuming that, in response to his proven ruthlessness, she'd accept his vastly superior experience and acquiesce to his demands with a grudging apology. Instead she'd gone on the attack, seizing the upper hand—a development he would never have envisaged—and for the first time in years he found himself on the back foot.

Silence bounced off the walls of the stairwell as their clashing gazes held, but the cacophony in his head was deafening. While the Sheikh's loyalty had never been in any doubt—although they'd be having dinner over his dead body—Olympia obviously hadn't made the link between the past and the present, between her family and his. So where did he go from here? Was he really going to have to explain that he didn't hate *her* exactly, but rather what she represented?

It would mean confessing that she looked so like her mother that every time he laid eyes on her he was seventeen again, trying to block out the arguments, the tears and the callous cruelty, and realising that life had changed irrevocably. He would have to reveal how deeply he resented constantly reliving not only the moment he'd found his father stone cold on the kitchen floor, a mere week after the divorce had been finalised, his hand still clutching his chest, but also his mother's later diagnosis of terminal cancer that he remained convinced had been brought on by everything she'd suffered. And, as if the prospect of exposing those vulnerabilities wasn't unpalatable enough, he'd also have to acknowledge the frenzied lust that she—Olympia—drummed up in him, which he loathed and feared in equal measure.

He too could recall the moment they'd met as if it were yesterday. The instant their gazes collided, he'd felt as if he'd been punched in the gut. Her smile had blinded him. The thunderbolt of desire that had gripped him had been so powerful, so consuming, he'd instantly understood how nations could be obliterated in the pursuit of it. Instinctively, he'd known that if he'd taken her hand in his, he'd have pulled her into his arms. He'd have crushed his mouth to hers, as if they were the last two people on earth and the survival of the human race depended on them doing something about it.

He'd never experienced such a threat to his control. Shocked to the core by the strength of his reaction to her—and horrified at the idea of history repeating itself, albeit a generation removed—he'd had to walk away. He'd had no choice. He would never succumb to such temptation. He could not contemplate the resulting chaos. He would not be that weak.

Ever since, he'd sworn to keep his distance. And he had. Until tonight, this very minute, when they were standing less than two feet apart, eyes locked, the bristling air that filled the space between them thickening and heating to such a degree that, suddenly, he couldn't recall what she'd asked.

His head was pounding and his heart was crashing against his ribs. Her proximity was stealing his wits. Despite who she was, and the threat she posed to his settled, well-ordered life, he wanted to yank her into his arms and propel her back against the deep-red silk-papered wall. To cover her with his body and his hands, until she was melting into him and sighing, clutching at his shoulders and moaning his name. When she touched the tip of her tongue to the corner of her mouth, the need to kiss her surged through him so fiercely, he actually had to hold himself back from leaning forwards and taking what he wanted.

'Ah,' she said, her voice penetrating the swirling fog in his head, with a breathlessness that made him think of twisted sheets and tangled limbs. '*Now* I get it.'

The knowing tone snapped him out of his trance. He stilled. Blinked. Focused on her face, finding her expression had lost the anger and challenge, and, after briefly flirting with astonishment, was now displaying baffling yet unsettling smugness. 'Get what?'

'You want me.'

Shock froze him to the spot. All the blood in his body drained to his feet. Surely he wasn't that transparent. Surely he hadn't actually *moved*. 'I beg your pardon?'

'You're attracted to me,' she said, running her gaze over him with a shrewd intensity that coated his skin in an ice-cold sweat, even as he burned. 'There's no point denying it. The evidence is indisputable. Your pupils are dilated. The pulse at the base of your neck is pounding. You couldn't take your eyes off my mouth just now. And I'm making an educated guess here, but I suspect that because you think so little of this *"pampered nepo princess"*—your words, as I recall—you don't want to want me. You desire me against your will and *that's* what you hate.'

For a moment, Alex couldn't think of a thing to say. He was utterly speechless. She was so appallingly right about everything, except *why* he didn't want to want her, that denial was his only option. 'Have you completely lost your mind?'

'Quite the opposite. The situation could not be clearer. And you know what I also think? I think this unwelcome desire you have for me is behind the grim, disapproving looks you've been shooting at me these past few months. They haven't just been about my scandalous reputation and the fact that my brother, the CEO, gave me a job for which I admit I have no experience. They've been because of you. You don't know how to handle me.'

His heart was beating so fast he felt as though he were about to pass out. 'That's quite a leap of the imagination.'

'Perhaps,' she agreed with a slight tilt of her head. 'But if I'm right—and I'm pretty sure I am—it would certainly explain what happened in the ballroom earlier.'

'How?' The word was out before he could stop it.

'You were jealous. Of the Sheikh. And I can see how it may have looked. We were standing fairly close together. That room has terrible acoustics. No wonder you were moved to stake your claim. He's a notorious womaniser.'

Beneath Alex's feet the floor shook. Rejection surged through him, blazing a scorching trail that singed the very marrow of his bones. *Stake his claim? What the hell?* Of course he wasn't jealous. Not only was jealousy a destructive, pointless emotion he'd never had any time for, but also it would mean he felt some sort of possessiveness towards

Olympia, which was so far out of the question it was in another galaxy.

Although it would explain the white-hot bolt of lightning he'd experienced when he'd first caught sight of her and the Sheikh talking. And the urge he'd had to break the other man's fingers when he'd seen him touch her. The flat denial that had surged through him at the thought of them having dinner too.

But no. All that had just been fury that she had the temerity to invade his space and was daring to try and create a professional rapport with someone she shouldn't. Nothing else. And the only claim he was interested in staking was on the Sheikh.

'This is insane,' he practically growled, the voice in his head nonetheless urging him to get the hell out now, while he still could, before he was pushed into doing something he'd regret, whatever that might be. 'You are completely deluded. And not nearly as irresistible as you seem to think. Not every man you meet is bewitched by your smile or succumbs to your charms. Some of us manage to remain immune. All *I* want is for you to stay out of my business.'

'So if I touched you, you'd feel nothing?'

Every muscle in his body tensed. 'Right.'

'I don't believe you.'

'I don't care whether you believe me or not.'

'Let's prove it, one way or another.'

Before he could even register her intention, she

stepped forward, closing the distance between them, and lifted a hand to his face, its destination evidently his jaw. But instinct kicked in—just in time—and he jerked his head away, catching her wrist in his hand. 'Stop this.'

'Stop this. Stop that,' she echoed, provocation dancing in her darkly amused eyes. 'You're very free with your diktats. Does everyone apart from me do what you say?'

Yes. They did. So how the hell had it come to this? To the two of them locked in a stand-off that she clearly expected him to lose? And how was he going to win it? He'd have to teach her a lesson she would never forget, a lesson that would make her regret ever deciding to take him on.

'Back off, Olympia,' he ground out, giving her one last chance to comply before facing the consequences.

'You first, Alex.'

'You're playing with fire.'

'So burn me.'

CHAPTER TWO

WHAT ON EARTH Olympia thought she was doing at this precise moment in time she had no idea. Twenty minutes ago she'd been trying to keep the Sheikh on the subject of investment and off dinner, while simultaneously wondering how much more of this she was going to have to endure. She was, of course, honoured to be representing Stanhope Bank at the conference this week, and would be eternally grateful that Zander had given her the chance to turn her car crash of a life around, but all this schmoozing was exhausting.

She'd been at it for six months now. Initially, she'd totally understood where her brother had been coming from when he'd told her that she needed to build up trust before she could start managing the funds their uber wealthy clients invested in. After a decade of generating headlines that went along the lines of *Olympia screws up Olympically*, she was well aware that that her scandalous reputation meant she had a lot to prove. Even if she hadn't read the incredulous press reports about her appointment, she would have known that her well-publicised stint in rehab didn't exactly inspire confidence. So she'd been only too happy to show Zander that she could be relied upon in whichever way he deemed fit. And if that meant using her outgoing personality and her notoriety to drum up new business, then that was all right with her.

Such had been her determination to succeed that she'd smashed the target he'd set for her first year in a quarter of the time. Since then, on a roll, she'd doubled the number of investors she'd lured to the bank. She was more than ready to step up and take on the fund management position she'd been after ever since unexpectedly catching the finance bug in rehab. She was champing at the bit to get started.

But frustratingly, Zander still seemed to have doubts about her suitability for the job, about how her reliability and trustworthiness were still publicly perceived, which was why she'd targeted the Sheikh this evening. A richer, higher-profile investor would be impossible to find. Should she manage to lure *him* to Stanhope's, her brother could not fail to recognise her talents and reward them. What more could she do to prove her dedication and persistence?

Of course, she hadn't considered the possibility of Alex bloody Andino showing up and putting a spanner in the works. But then why would she? They'd never crossed swords before, which had always been completely fine with her. She'd had no desire to seek him out any more than he had her. She could still feel the sting of his slight when she'd tried to introduce herself. The stunned disbelief that he had so rudely ignored her outstretched hand and stalked off, leaving her standing there—red-faced, smarting and feeling like a fool—had taken weeks to fade.

What was his problem? she'd wondered pretty much ever since. Everyone liked her. She made sure of it. So the fact that he very much didn't had stuck to her like a burr. That he *had* found her resistible— or so she'd thought—had sorely piqued her vanity.

But that hadn't crushed the desire that had struck her like a sledgehammer that evening, as she'd briefly stood before him, her gaze locked to his for that one charged moment. Which was pretty galling, but unfortunately, attraction didn't care how he felt about her, or his rudeness. All *that* had been able to focus on was the darkly masculine perfection of his features. The deep brown eyes and the straight blade of a nose. The chiselled jaw and the sensuous mouth that invariably tightened whenever their gazes collided.

Nor, unfortunately, had it lessened over time. This evening, when he'd barged into her conversation with his towering height, powerful physique and shoulders as broad as the Aegean, she'd almost swooned. She'd forgotten how incredible he smelled.

How weak her knees went at the spicy, woody notes of his seductive scent, which tugged at something deep inside her, making her want to get all up close and personal.

But by focusing on her outrage, which had fuelled through her when she'd realised what he was up to, she'd kept it together. She'd fought her corner and had had surprising fun doing so. Because, while he'd clearly expected her to crumple in the face of his displeasure and back off as he demanded, in fact, his antipathy had had the opposite effect. In response to the great waves of tension he radiated, and the forbidding stoniness of his expression, the devil in her had stirred. The prospect of locking horns with him had thrilled her. She'd felt more exhilarated, more alive than she had in a year, and very much up for the fight.

And then, having clocked the crackle of electricity that zigzagged between them—and the trouble he had keeping his gaze off her mouth when she'd deliberately touched her tongue to her lips to confirm her suspicions—she'd realised what the past six months' antagonism had *really* been about, and her outrage had drained away. In its place had flooded hot heady desire that begged to be satisfied. The more he'd denied it the more determined she'd been to prove it, to find out how explosive the chemistry that sizzled between them might be, how good they could make each other feel if they unleashed it.

But God, he was a hard nut to crack. Even now, with time and the world at a standstill, her bold challenge hanging between them, he still resisted—even though the hammering of her pulse beneath his fingers had to reveal the effect he had on her.

Excitement was thundering through her. With mere centimetres separating them, he dominated her senses. His eyes blazed and his heat enveloped her. His scent was scrambling her brain, his touch sending tingles down her arm, and all she wanted was his mouth on hers and his hands exploring her body. To experience the electrifying passion that she'd missed since reining in the wilder side of her character.

So maybe, because of the recklessness that was turning the blood in her veins to fire, she ought to shake herself free and step away. The mindfulness techniques she'd learned in rehab to ride out any disruption that might set back her recovery—any disruption to her composure at all, in fact—were so ingrained she could recall them at the drop of a hat, and she probably should. Besides, some sixth sense warned her that prodding this particular beast might not be wise.

But she wanted Alex's surrender more. She wanted to punish him for what he'd done back there in the ballroom. To finally win this battle of attrition he'd started. She longed to find out what would happen when his resistance cracked. So she deliberately lowered her gaze to his mouth and let it linger. She drew in a slow deep breath, which brought her aching breasts into contact with the solid wall of his chest, and held it.

For the longest time he didn't move a muscle. He didn't seem to be breathing either. And it was just beginning to occur to her that sickeningly, *mortifyingly*, maybe she'd got it all wrong and he didn't want her, when suddenly he moved. In the blink of an eye she was up against the wall, the air whooshing from her lungs. His head descended, blotting out the light, the stairwell, everything but him, and his mouth slammed down on hers.

Pinning her there with his big hard body, he took advantage of her parted lips to possess her in a kiss that was hot and ferocious, no doubt designed to establish his dominance and demonstrate that he was a dangerous man to trifle with. He instantly released her wrist to bury his hand in her hair, angling her head to increase the intensity with which he plundered her mouth, as if he didn't want to just burn her but brand her, as if he were aiming to imprint himself on her memory for ever.

And he was succeeding. She'd never had a kiss like it. Every one of her senses was under siege. Her brain was short-circuiting and her bones were disintegrating. She was losing her mind and her control, so much so that when he lifted his head a moment later and growled, 'I did warn you. I never bluff. I hope you've learned your lesson,' she actually whimpered in protest.

But if his intention had been to put her off with that punishing but thrilling onslaught it had backfired spectacularly. She wanted more. She wanted everything—danger, dominance, every dark desire he possessed. So he might be loosening his grip on her, making to step away, but he and his clever mouth were going nowhere.

Giddy with need, Olympia surged forwards, threw her arms around his neck and pulled his head back down to hers. Kissing him as fiercely as he'd just kissed her, she arched her back so that every quivering inch of her pressed against every shocked, rigid inch of him.

And then, there it was—the moment his control snapped—and it was as dramatic and exciting as she'd imagined.

His arms whipped around her, crushing her in a tight embrace that she couldn't have escaped if she'd wanted to, and her body went up in flames. His fingers were in her hair and his scent was in her head and in her blood, intoxicating her to the point of madness. Within seconds she'd become a pounding mass of lust, reduced to making little moans of pleasure at the back of her throat as he ground his pelvis into hers, his rock-hard erection digging into her right where she wanted him most.

He wrenched his mouth from hers to draw in a

ragged breath, then set his lips to her neck. As her head fell back to allow him better access, she trembled and gasped. He trailed hot kisses down the sensitive skin of her chest. As he did so, he tugged down the spaghetti straps of her dress. The soft shimmering fabric fell to her waist, exposing her bare breasts to his scorching gaze, and when his mouth closed over her nipple, her knees buckled.

In response to this delicious torment heat poured through her. The need to have him inside her consumed her. Shaking, mad with desire, she shifted to put a sliver of space between their lower bodies. Her hand found their way to the button of his trousers and his zip, moulding to his straining length in a move that she couldn't begin to claim was accidental.

Alex hissed out a harsh breath and jerked back. He pushed up her dress and, with her help, he yanked her underwear off. She tackled his trousers and shorts, shoving both down while he located his wallet, fished out a condom and rolled it on.

Using the wall for support, he planted his hands on her thighs and lifted her up, parting her legs, stepping between them as he did so. Panting desperately, clinging tightly to his shoulders, Olympia shifted her hips, and on a rough groan he surged into her liquid heat.

He held still for a moment, a stunning moment she used to familiarise herself with the exquisite feel of him, so big and deep inside her that she actually saw stars, and then, as she locked her legs around his waist, pulling him in even further, he began to move.

Their mouths met in a fiery clash of teeth and tongues. He didn't bother with slow and measured, but struck up a quick intense rhythm that she matched stroke for stroke. With every powerful thrust she lost a little bit more of her mind. The friction of her sensitised breasts against the crisp white cotton of his shirt sent such strong sparks of electricity to her nerve-endings that she thought she was about to combust.

She'd never felt such raw animal passion, such wild abandonment, and she never experienced it in someone else either. There was nothing tender and romantic about what they were doing. It was primal and electric. The fight for completion was instinctive, a mutual goal, a battle which, this time, they would both win. They were volcanically in synch. So much so that when she tore her mouth from his and bit into his jacket-clad shoulder, muffling her cries as she shattered powerfully around him, he buried his head in her neck, thrusting into her one last time, hard and deep, and climaxed so intensely that it detonated another explosion inside her.

For the longest moment, as the blazing pleasure ebbed and the heat cooled, all she could hear was the thundering of her heart and the raggedness of their breathing. She barely had the strength to open her eyes, let alone speak. But she just about managed when he eventually eased out of her and stepped back to set her on her feet.

'So that was wild,' she said dazedly, as she tugged her dress into place while he dealt with the condom, then pulled up his shorts and trousers and put himself back together. 'I thought it might be good, but I had no idea it would be *that* good. I've never experienced anything like it. You nearly blew the top of my head off. Want to find out what we could do in a bed?'

'No.'

The word shot from him like a bullet from a gun. Olympia stilled. She lifted her gaze to his face. Noting the rigid jaw and blank expression, she felt a tiny shiver of ice-cold apprehension run down her spine, and she frowned. 'What?'

His dark eyes glittered. Tension rolled off him in great buffeting waves. 'This shouldn't have happened,' he growled. 'We will never speak of it again.' And with that, he stalked to the door, yanked it open and vanished.

CHAPTER THREE

Eight weeks later

THESE PAST TWO MONTHS, never speaking of what she and Alex had done together in the hotel stairwell in Switzerland had suited Olympia down to the ground. Not even thinking about it—or him—had suited her even better, because with his parting shot, he'd turned the hottest ten minutes of her life into some of the seediest.

It wasn't that she had a problem with one-night stands. On the contrary, prior to going into rehab, she'd learned to favour ultra-casual flings, which gave her the rush she craved. She was far too screwed up to be trusted with a relationship, and who would ever want to take on her and her issues anyway? No strings meant no disappointment. No possibility of rejection. No danger of swapping one dependency for another and transferring her innate neediness onto a man.

Besides, she wasn't sure she even knew what love meant. She certainly hadn't received any from either of her parents. Before his fatal heart attack when she was nine, her aristocratic British father had been a stern distant figure, only interested in his heir—her eldest brother, Leo. Her scandalous Greek social-ite mother had never had time for anyone but her-self, and still didn't. And with five older siblings, she'd had to fight for every scrap of attention she'd been given, none of which could have been called unconditional.

It was the way the night had ended that left such a bad taste in the mouth. She'd thought she and Alex had been on the same page. He'd certainly demon-strated an equal degree of feral desperation. She hadn't had sex with anyone since checking into the clinic in Arizona, and she'd been excited by the idea of making up for lost time with him.

But he'd made her feel as though they'd done something shameful, something grubby. She'd been left with the impression that, bafflingly, not only did he deeply regret succumbing to desire, but also he held her to blame for his loss of control. His un-expected and inexplicable anger had winded her. His rejection had stung. Her brittle self-esteem had plummeted, and for the first couple of weeks she'd been back in Athens she'd hated him for all of it.

Nor was she all that keen on herself, if she was being honest. She still couldn't work out what on earth she'd been thinking that night. Acting on im-pulse had been one of the first problem areas that therapy sessions in rehab had identified. She'd spent weeks learning strategies to control it, and had put considerable effort into working on this particular flaw.

Yet the minute Alex had confronted her in all his thrillingly dark and handsome glory, she'd forgotten every single one of them. She hadn't questioned for one moment the wisdom of taking what she so badly needed. Had they been caught, the press would have had a field day. She'd have been fired on the spot, her fledgling career over, her improving but still fragile reputation in tatters.

However, none of that had crossed her mind. The second he'd pulled her against him and crushed his mouth to hers she'd been utterly lost. The flicker of triumph she'd experienced at his surrender had been burned to a crisp by the bonfire he'd lit. All she'd been able to focus on was taking what they were doing to its natural conclusion as quickly as possible.

Stupidly, unthinkingly, she'd positioned herself at the top of a slippery slope, at the bottom of which lurked a version of herself she was trying to put behind her. The reckless rebel, who'd taken attention seeking as a child to a whole new boundary-pushing level in adolescence, by first flirting with an eating disorder and shoplifting, then dabbling in drugs and alcohol and casual sex—bad choices all of them. She'd slipped back into old habits as if she'd never spent three months in Arizona working out why she behaved the way she did, then doing her best to create better, less destructive ways to measure her self-worth. She'd thrown caution to the wind and chased the high that would make her feel like a billion dollars without a thought to the consequences.

And now she was paying for it.

Because, as she'd discovered this Friday morning, half an hour ago, here at the clinic where she'd had an appointment to find out what was behind her chronic tiredness and bloating, there was indeed a consequence. The sort that developed over nine months and lasted a lifetime.

She was pregnant.

Not ill, not suffering from ultra-delayed cold turkey, but pregnant.

Olympia's head spun and her stomach churned as she stared at the black and white printout of her uterus, containing the recognisably baby-shaped blob, which she held with clammy fingers that had been trembling for the last twenty minutes. Surely the scanner had to be faulty. The blood tests wrong. Because how could it have happened? She and Alex had had sex just the once and they'd used protection. It didn't make any sense. Had there been a problem with the condom? An application issue? Or had they just been spectacularly unlucky?

More pertinently, what the hell was she going to do about it? She wasn't equipped to have a child. Up until a year or so ago, she'd lived her life entirely on her terms, and those terms had not been great. She'd barely been able to look after herself, let alone anyone else, and even though she'd moved on—she hoped—she was still a little fragile. Still at risk of screwing up if she wasn't careful. And then there was her budding career, her need to prove she had value and purpose outside of supplying the gossip columns with material. What impact would a child have on that?

But despite the inconvenient timing and her many concerns about her ability to cope, she wanted this baby instantly, with a surprising strength that had made her throat tight and her chest ache. She wanted someone to shower with love and affection and to receive it back. To do it right. Her child wouldn't suffer the parental neglect she had, she vowed as she concentrated on breathing in and out, slowly and deeply. Her child wouldn't be left to fend for itself in a sea of older siblings and an absence of guidance.

So there was only one solution. However much she might recoil at the idea of facing him again, she was going to have to tell Alex. He blew so hot and cold that his reaction to the news was anyone's guess, but this was as much his concern as it was hers, and she had no other support. She needed to know whether or not he wanted to be involved and, if he did, what that involvement might look like. Only then could she proceed.

She hadn't seen him since he'd disappeared through the fire door that night, attractively rumpled yet confusingly brutal. Unable to stand the thought of bumping into him, and feeling even worse about herself than she already did, she'd packed her bags and left the conference early the following morning. Thereafter, somehow, she'd managed to avoid him completely.

But that wasn't an option any longer. Nor was sticking her head in the sand and pretending all this would go away in time—it wouldn't. She had to face reality, put the past behind her and focus on the future. There was no point dwelling on the unpleasant manner in which he'd abandoned her. Or bearing a grudge against him for the situation she was in because after all, he was the one who'd taken responsibility for contraception. Regret and blame would help no one, least of all this new life they'd created.

What *would* help was staying cool and in control when she confronted him. Presenting him with the facts plainly and unemotionally and above all maturely. She would not allow lust to throw her off course again, she told herself as she carefully stowed the ultrasound in her handbag and pulled out her phone to try and track him down. Or any emotion for that matter. She would finally deploy the tactics she'd learned to curb her impulsive streak and rise above any unfathomable animosity he might still display towards her.

She had someone else to think about now, someone who needed her to make this work, whatever the sacrifice, and that was all that mattered.

Sitting at his desk in the office suite that occupied the entire penthouse of the twenty-storey Athens building, which housed Andino Asset Management, Alex was in the middle of mentally calculating the money he could potentially make by shorting the yen against the dollar, when one of his three assistants put her head around the door.

'Sorry to disturb,' Elena said with an apologetic grimace, 'but Olympia Stanhope is on her way up. I checked and she doesn't have an appointment. However, according to the receptionist she was very insistent on seeing you. She was threatening to make a scene. I thought it best to contain the situation by complying with her wishes.'

In response to this revelation, Alex barely moved a muscle. His gaze merely flickered from the screen in front of him to Elena, then back again, while his pulse skipped a beat and his brain screeched to a halt. He hardly even breathed.

Up until now he'd done an excellent job of blanking the appalling encounter he'd had with Olympia from his head. Even though it had been the hottest sex of his life, the last thing he wanted to do was revisit such a monumental loss of control with a woman who represented everything he detested, and not just because of her surname.

What the hell had he done? That was the question battering his thoughts as he'd stormed back to his hotel suite, still recovering from the most earthshattering orgasm he'd ever had, while simultaneously feeling sick to his stomach with self-loathing and regret, furious with himself, her, the entire bloody world. He'd allowed himself to be seduced by a self-proclaimed hedonist, a charming, beautiful scandal of a woman who wouldn't know responsibility if it slapped her around the face.

He should never have approached her that night. He should have waited until the morning, when she wouldn't have been wearing an aggravating dress and her thick glossy hair would have been up in its usual neat and tidy arrangement, instead of down in loose alluring waves about her shoulders.

But even as she'd demanded he burn her, he could have salvaged the situation. All he'd had to do was release his grip on her, take a step back and demonstrate supreme control by getting the hell out of there. Yet he hadn't moved. He'd been transfixed by the challenging jut of her chin and the knowing, teasing glint in her eyes. Then she'd deliberately brought her breasts into contact with his chest and all rational thought had vanished.

She needed to be shown that *he* was in control

here, he'd thought as he'd raked his gaze over her stunning face, the arch of one fine eyebrow, the hint of a provocative smile on her beautiful mouth. So if she wanted to be burned, he'd burn her. He'd brand her so deeply she'd run a mile whenever their paths crossed, riddled with regret that she'd ever decided to take him on.

But it was he who'd been branded. Because the minute he'd kissed her—in a mindbogglingly stupid attempt to teach her some sort of a lesson—he hadn't stood a chance. The desire he'd had for her was simply too overpowering. And it was his brain that had disintegrated when he'd finally pulled back and she'd thrown herself at him.

His defences reduced to rubble by her extraordinarily effective assault, he'd succumbed to temptation. He'd slept with the enemy. Which meant that not only had he made a mockery of his driving force these past two decades, but also that he was not nearly as strong-willed as he'd always assumed. In fact, he was just as weak as his father, incontrovertible proof that the apple really didn't fall far from the tree.

Who would want to recall any of that? He certainly didn't. Therefore he hadn't, and he was so single-minded that it hadn't even taken much effort. He'd just wiped the entire incident from his head, as if it had never happened, and that had been that.

However, now Olympia was here. Why, he had no

idea. But while instinct urged him to instruct Elena to get rid of her, logic told him that he couldn't turn her away. The scenes she made tended to end up on the front pages of newspapers, and his business could do without that sort of scandal.

And really, there was no need for alarm, he assured himself as the shock receded and his brain cranked back into gear. It wasn't as if he'd be blindsided by her effect on him again. He knew what to expect. He would not be hurled off track by memories of how incredible she'd felt in his arms or the soft little sounds she'd made as, together, they found oblivion. He would not look at her and suffer an attack of the past. Whatever she had to say, he'd hear her out, then respond appropriately with icy indifference and rock-solid immunity.

'Show her in,' he said, taking a moment to pre-pare himself, so that when she stepped into his office a moment later, he was able to bank the im-mediate response of his body to the sight of her, get-ting to his feet as if completely unmoved.

Pleasingly, he was so unaffected he barely noticed the mini earthquake she seemed to be setting off as she crossed the floor, or the rearrangement of the air so that it apparently no longer contained oxygen. He merely slid his hands into the pockets of his trousers and watched her as she came to a stop on the other side of his desk, somehow managing to make blue jeans, white trainers and a biscuit-coloured blazer over a white T-shirt look like haute couture.

'Good afternoon, Olympia,' he said, giving her the smallest of nods and allowing his mouth to curve into a faint but humourless smile. 'You just can't resist invading my territory, can you?'

'It's delightful to see you too, Alex,' she replied with equal cool.

'How have you been?'

'Just fine. You?'

'Couldn't be better. May I offer you something to drink?'

'No, thank you.'

'Please do take a seat.'

She sank elegantly into the chair he'd indicated while he sat back down, refusing to recall how the last time he'd seen her she'd been convulsing around him and biting his shoulder to muffle her cries of pleasure. 'Did you enjoy the last day of the conference?'

'I left early that morning.' She crossed her legs and linked her hands over her knee. 'Things to catch up on. I assume you didn't stay either.'

'I'd been away from the office long enough.'

'Of course.' She gave her head the tiniest of tilts and smiled. 'I must say, I've been surprised not to bump into you these past few weeks. You haven't been avoiding me, have you?'

'Not at all,' he said easily, thinking that of course

he hadn't been avoiding her. He'd simply been so busy with work recently he'd considered it a judicious use of resources to send others in his stead whenever Andino representation was required at an event. 'I've just had a lot on. As have you, I hear. I knew it was too much to hope you'd quit the industry entirely.'

'Sorry to disappoint.'

He arched one sceptically amused eyebrow. 'Are you?'

'Not remotely.'

'I didn't think so. At least you saw sense and backed off my business.'

'I had no choice. Your clients are mystifyingly loyal.'

'There's nothing mystifying about it. Not only do my results consistently outperform everyone else's, but I've also spent years building and curating the relationships I have. Why would anyone jump ship?'

'Yes, well, fortunately for me, others aren't quite so good at what they do.'

While Alex could admit he found this back and forth mildly entertaining, he doubted it was the reason she'd pitched up at his office. He was keen to find out what it was, so he could eject her from his building and move on with his life.

'So to what do I owe this pleasure, Olympia?' he asked, steepling his fingers as he continued to regard her impassively. 'What are you doing here?'

For a moment, she just looked at him blankly, as though she'd forgotten. Then she gave herself a quick shake, took a breath and said, 'I have some news.'

Oh? 'Couldn't you have called?'

'My phone was hacked once and it's the sort of news best delivered face to face anyway.'

A ripple of apprehension shivered down his spine. 'That sounds ominous.'

'It might be. Or it might not be. Depends on your perspective.'

'How cryptic.'

'You must be busy so I'll get to the point.'

Finally.

'I know we were supposed to forget all about what we did together the last time we saw each other and, believe me, I was fully on board with that. In fact, given the way you stalked off and left me there, I would have been perfectly happy never to lay eyes on you ever again. As an exit strategy, yours leaves a lot to be desired. But unfortunately, keeping out of each other's way is no longer possible.'

'Why not?'

'Because that night created a situation.'

'What sort of a situation?'

She pulled her shoulders back and looked him straight in the eye. 'I'm pregnant, Alex,' she said. 'And the baby's yours.'

CHAPTER FOUR

As THAT BOMBSHELL landed Alex stilled. The world skidded to a stop. Every muscle in his body tensed and his head spun. It was a good thing he was sitting down. Had he been standing he might well have keeled over.

But then, cold hard logic kicked in, scything through the shock, and told him no. Absolutely not. That didn't make any sense at all. So what was going on? What was she up to?

Shifting in his chair to get his blood flowing again, he pulled himself together and focused on the facts, which rendered her claim a lie. 'Is this some sort of a joke?'

Olympia's eyebrows shot up. 'A *joke*?' she said on a sharp intake of breath. 'Why on earth would I joke about something like this?'

'I have no idea,' he said with the shrug of one shoulder. 'To punish me for walking off that night in Switzerland? Because the papers need a story? For fun?'

'Are you *serious*?'

'Deadly.'

'I'm not that vindictive,' she said tightly. 'Nothing about any of this is fun or for a story. And it's very much not a joke. I had an ultrasound this morning.' She dug around in her bag for a moment and withdrew a small square of paper, which she thrust at him. 'Here's the photo. According to the doctor, I'm ten weeks along.'

He automatically took it and glanced down at the grainy black and white image below her name, which clearly showed a tiny human being floating in a circle of black. Which proved she was pregnant, but that was all.

'Congratulations,' he said, handing it back as if it were on fire. 'But I'm not the father. I can't be.'

'You can and you are. Unfortunately. Not only do the dates fit, but you're also the only person I've had sex with in over twelve months.'

'Do you honestly expect me to believe that, with your past?'

In response to his cutting tone she flinched minutely, but he refused to allow her reaction anywhere near his conscience. She was a Stanhope and therefore not be trusted. 'It's the truth.'

Ha. 'I used protection.'

'Evidently incorrectly.'

No. That was a preposterous suggestion. He had over twenty years' experience of practising safe sex and not once in that time had he been careless. Not once had there even been the hint of a scare. What Olympia was implying was unthinkable. 'It's impossible.'

'Statistically, it's not. Improbable, yes. Impossible? No.'

'So I'm just supposed to accept what you say?'

'Well, I was hoping you would. But I'm happy to arrange a paternity test if you wish.'

Feeling as though the walls were closing in on him, Alex didn't know what he wished. He couldn't think straight. He was finding it hard to breathe. There were spots in his vision. She was coolly pulverising every one of his objections, but he didn't want to concede she had a point about the statistics. He didn't want to acknowledge the growing feeling that she wasn't lying.

Yet for how much longer could he continue to ignore the evidence? Her ice cool façade was cracking. She looked to be as thrown by this as he was. She was unnaturally still and her face was pale. And what possible ulterior motive could she have for pressing him to acknowledge the paternity of her child? She wouldn't be after his money. She had plenty of her own.

So perhaps the unthinkable *wasn't* all that unthinkable. He'd been so crazed with need that night he'd barely been able to recall his own name. His hands had been shaking. He might well have deployed less haste and more speed. Or maybe the condom had split. He'd climaxed so hard it wasn't beyond the realm of possibility. All of which meant that he *could* be the father of this baby. And, more shockingly, if he was, then it was entirely his fault.

'However, I'm not here to assign blame,' she continued, her steady tone slicing through the storm swirling around his head and the nausea churning up his stomach. 'What's done is done, and thrashing out what went wrong seems pretty pointless. I realise it's a shock—it was to me too—but you *are* the father of my child. I'm here because I thought you should know, and to find out how much you want to be involved.'

'You're keeping it?'

'I am,' she said with a decisive nod. 'The circumstances could not be worse but I am. And what I'd like to know is, what do *you* want?'

Alex stared at her blankly. What sort of an idiotic question was that? He was still having trouble accepting the situation, despite the increasingly obvious truth of it, and he'd never felt so at sea. 'How the hell do I know?' he snapped, pushing back his chair and surging to his feet, overwhelmed by the need to move, to pace, to do something to ease the dawning realisation that, once again, life as he knew it was over. 'I haven't had any time to think about it.'

'I'm happy to wait while you do.'

How long did she have?

He scrubbed his hands over his face as if trying

to wake himself from a nightmare, and strode to the window through which there was a spectacular view of the Parthenon, not that he could focus on that right now.

Fatherhood wasn't something he'd ever contemplated before. For one thing, he'd never met anyone who'd remotely tempted him to do so, and for another, the mere thought of marriage and family brought him out in hives. He'd witnessed how fragile relationships could be, the devastation they could cause when they broke down, and he had no wish to either experience the direct pain himself or inflict it on others.

Nor did he have any truck with love. The implosion of his parents' marriage had taught him that the heart was fickle and not to be trusted. That handing responsibility for your own well-being and happiness to someone else to destroy was foolish beyond belief. It was best, he'd decided in the aftermath of that hideously acrimonious divorce, to avoid love and commitment at all costs, which was why he stuck to short-term, sedate, no-strings affairs that came to a mutually agreed end with no fuss and no drama.

What he'd done with Olympia had been anything but sedate, and she was drama personified. And it wasn't over, because with the birth of this baby—which he knew deep down in his bones had to be his—they would be connected for ever. He'd be constantly reminded of the year he'd had to grow up fast. Its grandmother would be Selene Stanhope, the viper that two decades ago had slithered into his family's nest and wrecked three lives. Leo— the best friend he'd brutally cut off out of a sense of self-preservation—would be its uncle. Of all the women he could accidentally get pregnant, Olympia had to be the absolute worst, not least because she drummed up in him the sort of uncontrollable, insatiable lust he despised.

And yet…

He couldn't deny the flicker of primitive excitement leaping about in the pit of his stomach at the notion of another being in this world with half his DNA. He would no longer exist on his own. He would have something else to channel his energies into, not just work. His bloodline would continue, his life would have evolutionary purpose and, in a way, the family he'd lost would be replaced. Instead of dwelling on the past he'd have a reason to look to the future, which was a confusingly appealing prospect.

The last of his resistance evaporated, and despite the many external complications to this particular pregnancy, an unexpected wave of protectiveness swept through him. Hot on the heels of that was the sharp realisation that there was no way he would allow Olympia to bring up his child on her own. She seemed to be on an even keel these days, if her absence from the gossip columns was anything to go by, but what if she relapsed? What if she wrecked things in some other way?

Furthermore, he was not having his child raised a Stanhope. He couldn't imagine a greater insult to his mother's memory, or a bigger mockery of his achievements. It would be an Andino, brought up on his values—whatever those turned out to be— and that was final.

Olympia had had him on the back foot and dangling from her strings since the moment they'd met, but that stopped now. He was taking control of the situation, nailing it down, so that if and when she screwed up he'd be there to minimise the fallout. To remove her from the picture altogether if it came to that. He would never let his child be subjected to the sort of devastation he'd suffered. Never. Nor could he ever allow a situation in which she waltzed off and cut *him* out of the picture.

So he didn't give a toss if she had a problem with 'the circumstances' as she so euphemistically put it. If he could rise above what her mother had done to his family then so could she. The new life she was carrying transcended his feelings towards the Stanhopes. He would do everything in his power to keep it safe.

Filled with steely resolve and flatly ignoring the voice in his head, which insisted there had to be some other solution because this one could prove a disaster in ways he couldn't even begin to comprehend, he turned to face her and announced, 'You and I will be married.'

In response to Alex's stunning and wholly unexpected solution, the tension that had been gripping Olympia ever since the doctor had revealed she was pregnant drained from her system so fast her head spun. The strength left her limbs, her vision blurred, and it was taking every drop of willpower she possessed to stay upright.

Oh, thank God for that, she thought, letting out a long steady breath as her head gradually cleared and her heart rate slowed. What a result. Some people, she knew, might take umbrage at the obsolete idea of marriage for the sake of a child. Others might baulk at the thought of being tied to someone they didn't know and didn't particularly like for ever.

Not her, though.

All she felt was relief. Blessed, overwhelming relief. Because, despite the continuing friction that existed between them—not to mention his unflattering denial of the situation, which she'd decided to attribute to shock and had therefore risen above—she didn't know what she would have done if Alex had told her she was on her own and turfed her out of his building. She hadn't realised how desperately she'd been relying on his support until she had it. And, quite frankly, that support could not have come in a better form than the one he'd just suggested.

Evidently he was intent on sharing the immense responsibility, which would have been enough on its own, but with this proposal of marriage the future would be secured. In the event she screwed up—entirely possible, despite the progress she'd made with her recovery—her baby would be safe.

Of course, nothing was ever guaranteed, but the set of his jaw and his steely tone indicated a reassuring degree of resolve, of commitment. Formalising their relationship would minimise the possibility of him abandoning them when the going got tough, and it would maximise the chance of making a success of things. So from that point of view, it was a no-brainer.

But it might also have further benefits, she had to admit as she rapidly worked through all the implications of embarking on such a course of action. Ones of considerably less significance, of course, but nevertheless appealing. It could be professionally advantageous. A public demonstration of stability and maturity. Proof that she'd put the past behind her for good and settled down. That, ostensibly, one person at least believed her to be trustworthy and dependable. He would give her gravitas and their union could be presented as a whirlwind romance culminating in a fairy-tale wedding. No one need ever know the true circumstances of the arrangement.

And there was no denying that the physical side of things would be thrilling. The events of today might have turned life for both of them on its head but, despite the shocking impact of this meeting, an undercurrent of attraction still sizzled between them.

When she'd walked in and seen him standing behind his desk, shirt sleeves rolled up, top button undone, watching her intently from behind a pair of black-framed glasses, she'd almost forgotten why she'd come. She'd been hit by the urge to push him down and settle herself on his lap. To set her fingers to his shirt and tackle the rest of the buttons. And he wasn't immune to her either. He hadn't taken his eyes off her once and, for all his stony indifference earlier, that pulse at the base of his neck still throbbed madly. Therefore, assuming he'd got over whatever had spooked him in the stairwell, she saw no reason why they shouldn't indulge that raging chemistry whenever the mood took them.

So what would be the downsides of agreeing to his suggestion? Well, for one thing, there was his surliness, which she was beginning to think was his default setting—at least when it came to her. But she would charm him out of that eventually. As she'd once told him, she could be remarkably persuasive, and she had no doubt that with a little effort she would have him eating out of her hand in no time at all.

Then there was the prospect of binding herself to him for the next twenty years or so, but it wasn't as if she'd be giving up some childhood dream or anything. Marrying for love, in the manner of her siblings, had never been on the cards for her. She'd done nothing to deserve that sort of happiness, had no idea what love even was, if she was being honest, and as everyone knew, she was a flighty, irresponsible good-time girl. Or at least she had been. Now she wasn't quite sure what she was, but that didn't matter. Career progression and optics aside, all that really mattered was the baby.

After years of doing everything wrong, now was the time to do what was right. And that was providing her child with the best possible life she could, the life she would have given anything to have had. So it was the easiest thing in the world to nod firmly and get to her feet. To straighten her spine, smile brightly and say, 'Great!'

And when he told her 'I'll be in touch' as he walked her to the door, she was so giddily relieved about how well this had all worked out she didn't even wonder how.

CHAPTER FIVE

AT TEN THE following morning, Alex had just emerged from the pool when he heard the roar of an engine somewhere in the vicinity. Irritated beyond belief by the potential intrusion into his privacy, he slung a towel round his neck, then flung open the front door and strode out into the wince-inducing sunshine. A nifty red convertible was zooming up the drive. He didn't recognise the car but he sure as hell recognised its occupant, and the instant he did, the tension he'd worked off by ploughing up and down the pool for an hour returned with a bang.

He had not slept well. Yesterday afternoon, unable to concentrate on anything in the aftermath of Olympia's life-altering news—and utterly drained of the adrenaline that had sustained him throughout their conversation—he'd had his driver bring him home. On arrival, he'd headed straight to his study and cracked open a bottle of *tsipouro*. Then he'd thrown himself into an armchair and had steadily worked his way through it while raking over the cataclysmic events of the day.

What on earth had just happened? was the question he'd asked himself repeatedly as he'd stared out of the window into the twilight, four glasses in. Could he have dreamed the whole thing? It hadn't seemed real. Olympia's ready acceptance of his marriage proposal, all the more remarkable for the absence of defiance, had certainly lent the encounter an air of fantasy.

But no. He hadn't, of course. After years of studiously avoiding any sort of emotional tie, one misstep and he'd suddenly acquired a very real wife-and-child-to-be. What was he going to do with them? How was he going to be able to face the constant reminder of her mother and the damage she'd done? Would he ever get past it? Was there any chance— any chance at all—that this was all some catastrophic misunderstanding?

Unfortunately, the industrial strength alcohol had supplied no answer to these or any of the other questions rocketing around his brain. Nor had it granted him the oblivion he'd sought. All it had done was give him a pounding headache and nightmares that tangled the present with the past, then woke him up, drenched in a cold sweat, his heart thundering so hard it was in danger of cracking a rib.

As a result, he was exhausted and woolly-headed and very much not up to Olympia ambushing him on his doorstep. But it was way too late to pretend he wasn't in, so once again, he'd just have to find out what she wanted and then send her on her way—a plan that today, unlike yesterday, *would* work.

'Good morning, Alex,' she said, briefly raking her gaze over him with a scorching intensity that made him wish he'd pulled on a shirt.

'That's debatable,' he muttered, feeling as if he'd gone up in flames. She got out of the car and, with a slam of the door behind her, marched round to the back. 'What the bloody hell is going on? How did you know where I live?'

'Friends in low places.'

With growing alarm he watched her pop the boot and duck her head, then heave out a small suitcase and plonk it on the cobbles.

'As for what's going on, isn't it obvious? I'm moving in.'

At that, his brows crashed together in a deep frown. His pulse skipped a beat and then began to pound. 'What?'

'I'm moving in.'

'Here?'

'Yes. Of course here. Where else?'

'No,' he said with a sharp shake of his head. 'Absolutely not. This is not what we agreed.'

'I don't remember discussing it at all,' she said dryly. 'Or any of the practicalities of the arrangement, as a matter of fact. And I know you said you'd be in touch, but it occurred to me earlier that we didn't even exchange phone numbers, which was why I couldn't call ahead.' She delved back into the car and extracted a holdall that she dropped next to the suitcase. 'But we do need to hammer out how this thing is going to work. And get to know each other. I live in the city centre. You live out here. A forty-minute drive between us isn't conducive to anything. You must agree cohabitation makes sense.'

Alex's teeth clenched and his head began to throb again. 'I do not have to agree to anything of the sort,' he said, never regretting more that they hadn't exchanged numbers. He did not have the where-withal to cope with this level of face-to-face assault.

'Well, I guess you could move in with me if you really object to me being here,' she said with a thoughtful tilt of her head. 'My apartment isn't as big as this, naturally, but it would suit equally well.'

At that scenario, a shudder ripped through him. God, no. Willingly enter Stanhope territory? That would be even worse. What if her mother showed up? 'It's out of the question,' he said, weak at the very thought of coming face to face with the selfish narcissistic socialite he held responsible for the detonation of his family. 'All of it.'

'There you go again with the diktats.'

'It's not happening.'

'Why not?' One fine dark eyebrow rose, yesterday's compliance evidently a blip. 'What's the problem? Why would you not see this as an excellent idea, and one that should be implemented right away? I do. I've even taken the next two weeks off work for that very purpose. I admit this situation isn't exactly ideal, but surely we have to make the best of it.'

Not ideal? That had to be the understatement of the century. And as for making the best of things, well, that wasn't happening. At least, not right now. Because for one thing he hadn't yet had the time or the headspace to work it all through. And for another, he couldn't have her in his vicinity until he'd figured out how to get a grip on his response to her once and for all.

Despite his excellent intentions yesterday, he'd still wanted to spread her across his desk and divest her of her clothing. And today, it was bad enough she was standing on his drive in a short yellow sundress, which clung to her curves and revealed far too much sun-kissed skin over long toned limbs for his peace of mind. He didn't dare imagine what might happen if they found themselves in close proximity to a bed. Sure, he could *try* and convince himself that he was particularly susceptible to her allure this morning because he wasn't firing on all cylinders, but the inconvenient truth was that he was *always* susceptible to her allure, and handling it required a plan that he had not yet devised.

Besides, they did not need to get to know each other. This marriage was to be purely practical. There'd be logistics to consider, of course, but a heart-to-heart that would likely strip him of his armour and bare his soul? No, thanks. And as for learning her innermost secrets, that appealed even less than spilling his. Every fibre of his being recoiled in horror at the prospect of forming an emotional connection with anyone, let alone a Stanhope. No one but a fool would willingly put himself in a position that could lead to pain and suffering and destruction so cataclysmic it took years to pick up the pieces.

And anyway, where had all this urgency sprung from? Was he missing something? Had he been too quick to shelve his concerns about her trustworthiness? Could she have an ulterior motive that had nothing to do with money? If so, what could it be? This was all happening too fast, and he now felt a pressing urge to slow it down. 'Perhaps I would like that paternity test, after all.'

'Really?' she said, sounding thoroughly unimpressed as she planted one hand on her hip and gave him a withering look. 'I'm more than happy to arrange one if you insist, but I thought that was settled.'

'You think a lot of things.'

'Why on earth would I be here if I wasn't one hundred per cent sure you are my baby's father? I'm not a masochist.'

She had a point. And deep down he didn't need a paternity test when the evidence was overwhelming.

He was just desperate to regain some sort of control over a situation that had none. 'So what's the rush?'

'What's the point in delaying?'

'The baby won't be born for another seven months. Only then will we need to make a decision about the future. You should withdraw your request for leave.'

Her eyes narrowed and her chin came up. 'So are you saying that we won't be married right away?'

Alex pinched the bridge of his nose and fought for calm. Quite honestly, he hadn't a clue what he was saying. He needed some time, dammit. All he *did* know was that, right now, he was getting what he wanted, which was her off his property and out of his head.

'What I mean,' he said, injecting some ice into his voice, so she could be absolutely clear about who was in charge, 'is that *I* will decide what is happening when. As you intimated yesterday, this situation is most likely my fault and it is therefore up to me to fix it. And when I have come up with a plan, believe me, you will be the first to know.'

'How?'

'Ring my phone.' He gave her his number, watched her dial it and somewhere in the depths of the house he heard the device ring. 'There. No more excuses to show up without invitation. Now go home.'

'And do what?' Olympia reached up to close the boot, her luggage still unfathomably on the ground.

'I don't care.'

'I have a better suggestion. Why don't you work on your plan while I settle in?' she asked, her mollifying tone scraping across his nerve-endings as much as her complete disregard for his instruction to leave. 'Better still, why don't we work on it together? I appreciate your willingness to accept the blame for this but, don't forget, I was there too. This is on both of us. There's no need to be noble.'

'I'm not being noble,' he said through gritted teeth, torn between physically removing her and her luggage from his drive and wishing fervently that he *could* forget. He might have done an excellent job of wiping that night from his brain for the last two months, but seeing her again yesterday had brought it all flooding back, in vividly appalling detail. 'There's nothing noble about any of this.'

'Marrying for the sake of a child is.'

'I simply wish to guarantee my rights.'

'Me too.'

'You already have all the rights.'

'You misunderstand,' she said. 'I want to guarantee *your* rights. I'm under no illusion that I won't mess this baby thing up. I'm hardly the most responsible person on the planet. Not all that long ago I was out every night, partying hard and throwing as much alcohol down my throat as I could. I haven't had a drink in a year, but people do relapse and I'm not so naïve or arrogant as to believe I might not be one of them. This child deserves to have at least one functioning parent, which is why I agreed to the marriage you proposed. I can't risk you disappearing the minute things get a bit tough.'

'There is no danger of that,' he said, thinking it was about the only thing he *was* sure of right now. 'I am fully committed to the baby we've created.'

'Prove it, then. Like I am, by being here, when in all honesty I'd rather be anywhere else. You do realise that I'm not the only one who's going to have to make sacrifices, I hope.'

In response to that very valid observation, what remained of Alex's weakened resistance collapsed. This wasn't about him, he realised with a jolt. This was about their child, and ultimately nothing else mattered. He would never do anything to jeopardise its well-being, so he had to put his misgivings to one side and bury his unfortunate attraction to its mother. He had to do what was best for *it*. And she might think that meant finding out about each other, but he had different ideas.

First of all, while he was certain of his commitment to the situation, he couldn't be certain of hers. She talked about sacrifice and prioritising their child, but from what he'd read she had a history of prioritising herself, and he'd witnessed her recklessness first-hand. What if she changed her mind about his involvement? What if she decided against the marriage and disappeared? He couldn't risk that happening, so forget waiting. Whatever it took, however much it cost, he'd marry her the instant he could arrange it.

Secondly—and concurrently—he would take action to mitigate the vulnerabilities she'd revealed. It was admirable that she recognised her weaknesses, of course, but they were clearly still a cause for concern. So, in addition to preparing the paperwork required for their union, he would have a watertight prenuptial agreement drawn up that would grant him sole custody in the inevitable event she screwed up. His child would never know danger or uncertainty, he vowed. It would never suffer because of the selfish actions of a parent, and if he ever had cause to enforce such a clause he would *relish* the opportunity of denying Selene Stanhope access to her grandchild.

Thirdly, he'd be controlling the narrative from this moment on, so that he could not be suckerpunched again, starting with a phone call to her brother and his former friend to explain the situation before anyone else could, therefore minimising further Stanhope hassle.

And finally, he was rapidly coming to the conclusion that while all this was rumbling away in the background, despite the severe personal discomfort it was going to cause him, he was going to have to move Olympia in. As if her actions in Switzerland weren't proof enough, showing up here unannounced further indicated she was a loose cannon, liable to go off without warning. Who knew what else she might get up to left to her own devices? Very soon they'd be married, and he wouldn't have his reputation tarnished by hers.

And it would be fine, he assured himself, forcing himself to adjust to the idea of allowing the enemy into his lair for the sake of their child. He could keep a lid on the mad desire he had for her. He'd faced tougher challenges. He was sure of it, even if he couldn't think of one at this precise minute. Once he'd given her a quick tour, he'd install her in a guest room as far from his own suite as it was possible to get. With any luck he would hardly notice she was there.

Already feeling more alert with the development of a strategy, and ignoring the myriad doubts still trying to barge their way into his head, Alex strode forward to pick up her bags. He stalked to the front door and turned when he reached it. With a tight smile, he gestured for her to go ahead and said, through teeth that were hardly gritted at all, 'Welcome to my home.'

CHAPTER SIX

WELL, *THAT* VERY nearly hadn't gone according to plan, Olympia thought as she walked past Alex, into the house, nodding distractedly when he dropped her luggage and instructed her to give him a moment before disappearing. Although, to be fair, she hadn't exactly had a plan. The minute she'd come up with brilliant idea of moving in, she'd messaged the firm that handled her family's security. Once she'd had his address, she'd packed her bags and hopped in the car. There hadn't seemed much point in hanging about. There never did.

When she'd swung off the main road and onto the drive, she'd taken one look at the house and decided that there were worse places to hang out for the next couple of weeks while she got to know the father of her child. On the ground floor, four windows extended out from either side of the elegantly pillared porch. On the first, nine windows spread across the entire width of the house. The symmetry was as soothing as the softly swishing trees that lined the drive, and the lush verdant lawns it bisected.

Of course, the pleasing sense of tranquillity had not lasted long. But in light of the conflict that had characterised every one of their encounters to date perhaps she should have anticipated Alex's resistance. It wasn't as if he'd ever made any secret of it, and it had been very much in evidence out there on his drive. At one point, she'd actually thought he'd been about to fling her luggage back into the boot, bundle her into the passenger seat and push her off. But he was the one who'd suggested marriage in little more than the blink of an eye. If she'd given it any thought she'd have assumed he'd got over the problem he had with her.

Evidently he hadn't. Or perhaps he simply didn't appreciate being caught unawares, which, if she was being brutally honest, hadn't had to be the case. She could have easily got his number from the same security firm that had provided his address. It would have certainly smoothed the way. But, although the thought of doing just that had briefly flitted across her mind, in some deep dark corner of her psyche she was aware that interesting things happened when his guard was down. She found riling him thrilling. Had she forewarned him, she most likely wouldn't have been presented with his semi-naked body, which would have been a shame.

When he'd stormed out of his house in nothing but black swim shorts, and a small white towel slung round his neck, she'd practically swallowed her tongue. Such broad shoulders. So many hard defined muscles. She'd taken one look at all that masculine perfection and been hit by an image of him in the pool from which he'd evidently emerged, scything magnificently through the water. She'd recalled how easily he'd lifted her against that wall in Switzerland, and had very nearly swooned all over again. When one mesmerising rogue droplet had trickled down his neck and then his pec, she'd wanted to lick it off and not stop there. And God, she could not *wait* to win him round and get her hands on him.

'This is a spectacular property,' she said, deciding to strike while the iron was hot when he returned to show her around, having disappointingly donned a shirt. 'Have you lived here long?'

'Ten years.'

'And before that?'

'An apartment in the city centre.'

As he took her through the myriad rooms on the ground floor she peppered him with more questions, which were also minimally answered. But her aim was to learn more about him and she was not to be deterred. 'Where did you grow up?' she asked in the second of the three reception rooms, which had French doors onto the terrace.

'Not far from here.'

'Do you have any siblings?'

'No.'

'Parents?'

'They both died a long time ago.'

'So you're all alone in this world.' She ran her fingers over the soft worn leather of a wingback chair, then glanced over to see how he felt about that.

'I won't be in seven months' time.'

'Neither of us will,' she said, frustratingly unable to discern anything from his inscrutable expression. 'It's going to be quite an adventure.'

'That's one way of describing it.'

'What if we mess up?'

'*I* won't.'

At the inference that she would, Olympia felt a flicker of hurt, which was inexplicable when that was something she herself had implied, so she determinedly shook it off. 'You might,' she said, turning her attention to the books on the shelves, just in case her face reflected the lingering sting. 'It happens.'

'Not to me,' he said with enviable confidence as he strode past her and opened the patio doors. 'Whatever the personal sacrifice, there are no lengths I won't go to for my child. I will do everything in my power to protect him or her. Of that you can be sure. Let's move to the garden. I could do with some air. Mind the step.'

Later, as she unpacked her things in the light and spacious guest room Alex had shown her, before stalking off as if he had the hounds of hell snapping at his feet, Olympia reflected on the aspects of their conversation that had stuck in her mind.

If he followed through with his promise, their child would be lucky indeed. No one had ever looked out for her. She'd had to fight her own battles and she hadn't done a very good job of it. He seemed as determined as she was that that fate would not befall her child. It strengthened her conviction that she'd done the right thing by coming here.

But a desire to defend and protect might not be the only thing they had in common, she thought as she hung up a dress. Could he be as troubled by loneliness as she was? Was professional success enough or did his chest sometimes ache with emptiness? He had no one, she had everyone, yet she'd never felt as alone as when she was surrounded by people. So perhaps this marriage could be good for them—not just as prospective parents but also as individuals. Perhaps, in time, they could provide each other with companionship. That was something she'd never had before. Had he?

But oh, she had to be careful, she reminded herself as she carried her toiletries into the bathroom and decanted them into the vanity unit. She must not make the mistake of reading more into this than there really was. The marriage proposal, agreeing to cohabit and his solicitousness over the step into the garden weren't for *her* benefit. *She* didn't matter to him. The baby did, as he'd pointed out in no uncertain terms, and it would do her no good at all to forget it.

The sound of her phone ringing jolted her out of these oddly turbulent ruminations and she returned to the bedroom to fish it out of her bag. It was Leo, her eldest brother, calling, no doubt, from Santorini where he built luxury yachts—and lived with his wife, Willow, and their two daughters—and quite honestly, his timing could not be more perfect. She could apprise him of the situation before he found out some other way. She could take the opportunity to spin what had happened as that whirlwind fairy-tale romance she'd decided on yesterday, ostensible proof that she was capable of a mature relationship with someone who wanted her, instead of the rather tawdry truth that was a regrettable one-night stand and faulty contraception. As long as she remembered to keep her feet firmly on the ground, where was the harm?

Dropping into the armchair that sat in front of the large window, overlooking the inviting pool and verdant gardens, Olympia swiped right.

'Hi, Leo,' she said brightly, all in all really rather satisfied with the way the morning was playing out, given the circumstances. 'How are you and Willow and my gorgeous nieces?'

'We're all fine.'

'Great. Good.' She shifted in the chair and braced herself. 'I'm glad you rang,' she said, her heart beating a little faster than usual, even though she totally had this. 'Because I have news.'

'That you're pregnant and getting married?' her brother said dryly. 'I heard.'

She stilled and frowned, the world momentarily tilting on its axis. What on earth? Surely that wasn't possible. It had been less than twenty-four hours and she hadn't told a soul. 'How?'

'I just had a call from Alex. I would offer you my congratulations, but as I understand the situation, it's not that sort of an arrangement. I'm ringing to find out if you're genuinely all right with it. He seemed to think you were, but say the word and I will ruin him.'

Her frown deepened and her blood chilled, the wind whipping from her sails as she absorbed this information. Alex had called her brother? Why would he have done that? How did he even have his number? *She'd* wanted to be the one to tell her family her news, dammit. The needy attention-seeking kid she'd once been, traces of whom still lurked deep inside her, had been looking forward to Leo's reaction. To *her* version of events, which presented her in the best light—not the truth, which didn't.

'What did he tell you?' she asked, trying to keep her voice steady, although confusion, distress and her rising anger at Alex ripping the rug from under her feet made it hard.

'That you'd had a one-night stand, which has resulted in a pregnancy, and you'd both agreed to get married for the sake of the baby. I must admit it came as quite a shock.'

Olympia's throat tightened and her head buzzed. 'Well, you know me,' she said, just about managing to inject some faux levity into her voice. 'Reckless, impulsive, always getting into trouble. Surely you couldn't have been *that* surprised.'

'I didn't mean that,' Leo said with what sounded like a tut. 'Your personal life is none of my business and none of us escaped our upbringing unscathed. As the youngest you must have suffered the worst of it, but you're really turning things around. It's impressive. And don't forget, Zander knocked Mia up after a one-night stand so your predicament isn't exactly unique. What I meant was that I haven't spoken to the guy in twenty years. It was quite the blast from the past.'

Oh. Right. Well, it was good to know that she wasn't being judged for what she'd done, although she was rather taken aback by the notion of Leo thinking her impressive. But, hang on a moment... A blast from the past?

'Do you *know* him?' she asked, her curiosity piqued despite the volatile emotions swirling around inside her.

'Well, I *did*, once upon a time,' Leo replied. 'We used to be friends. Best friends, in fact. But then our mother had an affair with his father and that put an end to that. You probably don't remember the summer I was so angry with Selene that I deliberately dashed her favourite yacht against the rocks. I was sixteen. You must have been about six.'

Olympia racked her brains, a process that was hampered by the impact of this major new piece of information Alex had never thought to mention. 'That does ring a bell,' she managed eventually, dimly recalling the one and only time their father had raised his voice, a remonstration against his eldest son and heir for his unacceptable display of irresponsibility.

'I'm not surprised Alex cut me off,' her brother continued. 'I'd have done the same in his shoes. Still, it took me a while to get over it. Strange how our paths haven't crossed since. I guess they will now. I'm pleased old wounds have healed.'

But had they? she wondered, her head now spinning with questions as the implication of Leo's revelations registered. What if she'd been wrong about Alex's issue with her? What if it had nothing to do with her reputation and nepotism and therefore wanting her against his will and everything to do with her surname? Was he the type to bear a grudge? Could he be out for revenge? Was she simply a pawn in some greater game?

Or was she getting carried away, her imagination going into overdrive? It had been twenty years. Surely it was all water under the bridge. He couldn't be that Machiavellian, could he? There was only one way to find out.

'Well, I appreciate the call,' she said, surging to her feet and stalking across the bedroom to the door, her heart thumping hard. 'And rest assured I'm fine with everything. Please give my love to Willow and the girls. But right now, I really have to go.'

If Alex had known how disturbing giving Olympia a tour of his house was going to be he would never have suggested it. He'd have left her to figure out what was where on her own, because almost immediately the reality of having her in his house had hit home.

First, there'd been questions about his family to head off. He didn't want to dwell on the past. He didn't want to think about the beautiful villa where he'd grown up, which had been built by his great-great-grandfather one hundred and fifty years ago, in his family ever since and then lost in the divorce. He had no doubt that with her determination to get to know him there'd be many more questions to come, and he did not relish the energy he'd have to expend in deflecting them.

Then, there'd been the surge of curiosity he'd experienced at the idea of her feeling as on her own in this world as he did. How was that possible when she had family and friends galore? Surely she was anything but lonely. And why did it warm something cold and hard inside him to know that if she was, then they had something in common beyond the baby they'd created? It made no sense. He wasn't looking for any sort of emotional connection. It was deeply unsettling.

Last but by no means least was the way she'd moved around his space that, up until that moment, had been his sanctuary, his escape from the demands of the city and other people. When she'd run her hands over the furniture, he'd imagined them on his body. She'd examined the books on the shelves and the art on the walls and he'd wondered what she thought of them. After successfully avoiding the Stanhopes for two entire decades, there one had been, pregnant with his child, nosing around his things, and it should have felt like a gross invasion of privacy, a betrayal even, but it hadn't. It had felt somehow right. And that had sent him into such a spin of bewildered appal that he hadn't been able to get the tour over and done with fast enough.

As soon as he'd parked her in a guest room tucked away at the far end of the house's east wing, he'd buried his alarming response to her presence here, which he didn't understand, and turned to the practicalities of the situation, which he did. He'd instructed his legal team to get cracking with the paperwork required for their marriage and the prenup that would protect his child—and him—against any future whim of its mother. He'd then requested that Elena send him a contact number for Leo Stanhope, and when it had come through a mere couple of minutes later he'd called it.

The ensuing conversation had been unexpectedly difficult, he reflected with a frown as he set about making some much needed coffee. He'd embarked upon it with the intention of delivering the news, dealing with any fallout and moving on. He had not anticipated being bombarded with memories of that time. Or, horror of all horrors, *feelings*.

When the affair had come to light all those years ago and his family had begun to implode, he'd been battered by a wide range of emotions. Confusion at what was going on. Guilt over the fact that he'd introduced Selene into his family by way of his friendship with Leo. Resentment that his life had been upended because, regardless of how it had started, his father hadn't been strong or honourable enough to put his marriage and his family above such basic, primitive lust. And then anger, grief and despair as the repercussions continued.

He'd assumed he'd let go of everything apart from the deep burning hatred for the woman he held entirely responsible for it all, who'd casually ended the affair when someone else caught her eye, and still wafted about in this world causing chaos while his parents lay cold in their graves. But the minute he'd heard Leo's voice on the other end of the line, the emotions had flooded back, suddenly bubbling away so dangerously close to the surface that he'd very nearly hung up. He hadn't resorted to such theatrics, of course—he was far too in control of himself for that—and he'd imparted the news as intended, but he'd nevertheless been disconcerted enough to agree to a drink and a catchup.

However, at least it was done. And he could easily get out of any social engagement, he assured himself, noting a shift in the air and glancing up to see Olympia marching into the kitchen, her jaw set and her dark eyes flashing in a way that was becoming only too familiar. He and Leo might have been best friends once, but those days were long gone. He had no interest in rekindling the relationship. He didn't do friends now anyway. He had far too much on his plate with work.

'All settled in?' he asked, ignoring the perverse thrill he felt in response to her evident and intriguing umbrage.

'Yes.'

'Do you have everything you need?'

'The room is very comfortable. Your baby thanks you.'

'It's welcome,' he said and stamped out the part of him that unfathomably wanted her gratitude too. 'So what's wrong?'

She came to a stop at the enormous island that stood in the middle of the room and hopped onto a stool. 'You called my brother and told him I was pregnant and we were getting married.'

Ah. Right. He should have guessed that Leo would be straight on the phone to his sister. He'd always been the loyal, protective sort. Alex had lost count the number of times the guy had got him out of sticky situations when they'd been friends. He recalled that Leo had once told him he'd rescued a five-year-old Olympia out from the bottom of a pool when she'd fainted during a swimming gala and no one had noticed. Earlier, his former friend had demanded to know if he—Alex—had some-how forced his sister into this marriage, which was so far from the truth it would have been laughable if any of this was remotely amusing.

'I did,' he said with a short nod as he leaned back against the worktop, folding his arms across his chest. 'Is that a problem?'

'Yes, it's a problem,' she said tightly. 'It was my news to share—not yours—and I had a plan.'

'How could your plan have differed to mine?'

'Yours was the truth, mine was not.'

His eyebrows rose. 'You were planning to lie to your brother about us?'

'You don't have siblings,' she shot back, her col-our high and her shoulders stiff. 'You wouldn't un-derstand the dynamics.'

'Try me.'

'I'm the youngest. The screwup. The one who's al-

ways courting trouble and attracting negative headlines. But I've been trying to change, to put my past
behind me, and I've been doing a very good job of it.
And, all right, so I slipped back into old habits with
you and what we did, and now there's this—' she
waved a hand in the direction of her abdomen '—but
when life gives you lemons you have to make lem-
onade, right? I was planning to turn a negative into
a positive and dress this up as a fairy-tale romance
in which I came out looking good. It was going to be
a chance to cement my reputation as a mature adult
capable of real responsibility. You just ruined that.'

Ignoring the flare of curiosity triggered by the
brief insight into her history, Alex focused instead
on the chill that was settling over him. With everything else going on he'd forgotten her capacity
for creating drama. Her addiction to the limelight
seemed to be embedded in her DNA. Her willing-
ness to manipulate the situation to suit herself made
him think of her mother and the destruction she'd
caused. If he'd needed a reminder of the importance
of keeping Olympia at arm's length, here it was.

'I apologise.'

'It's too late for that,' she said tartly. 'The damage is already done. Would *you* like people knowing you knocked someone up in a hotel stairwell?
How would your clients take that, do you think?'

He felt the urge to tell her not to speak of what
had happened like that, but because he had no clue

why he ignored it. 'They're all about the bottom line and I'm not remotely bothered by what people think of me.'

'Hmm. Well. Aren't you the lucky one?'

'Luck doesn't come into it. I've worked insanely hard for everything I have.'

'And I haven't, I suppose.'

'Have you?'

'I'm *trying*. And anyway, you're hardly one to cast judgement on honesty.'

'What do you mean by that? I'm not the one distorting the truth to further my own ends.'

'My mother and your father. Why didn't you ever mention they had an affair?'

He frowned, his blood icing over in the way it always did when that particular memory was jogged. *She didn't know? How was that even possible?* 'I assumed you knew.'

'I was six at the time, apparently. Why *would* I know?'

'Were there no arguments?'

'None at all. There never were about anything. My parents barely spoke to each other. They were hardly ever in the same room. How they managed to produce the six of us is a mystery. And it's not as if such a thing would have raised any eyebrows. Selene had affairs all the time and still does. Your father was one of so many I couldn't even begin to count them all. Leo mentioned crashing a boat, which I do vaguely recall, but I don't remember if your name came up. He said you cut him off. Why did you do that? What happened wasn't his fault.'

To some extent, Alex recognised the defensiveness in Olympia's tone, evidence of the same protective streak that Leo possessed, but it barely pierced the white noise rushing through his head. All of a sudden his heart was beating fast and hard. His chest was so tight he was struggling to breathe. An event that had been cataclysmic for the Andinos had caused hardly a ripple for the Stanhopes. While his life had been falling apart they'd just carried on as usual, and now she was hammering questions at him as if he were to blame for the fallout.

His vision blurred and a wave of nausea rolled through him. He wasn't ready to talk about it. He never would be. Not with her, not with anyone. He couldn't have her digging around in his psyche. He didn't need her opinion or her censure. He had to de-escalate this before he wound up telling her everything and exposed himself to carnage.

'It happened twenty years ago,' he said, ruthlessly suppressing all the roiling emotion until his pulse had slowed and he could breathe more easily. 'I was seventeen. Little more than a kid. I can hardly recall anything about it either.'

She tilted her head and narrowed her eyes at him. 'Are you sure?'

'Why wouldn't I be?'

'Selene's left a trail of angry spouses in her wake. Why not a clutch of angry children? Maybe you're using me to somehow get back at her. I do look like her, after all.'

'That's ridiculous,' he said, choosing to ignore the fact that the resemblance had occasionally spooked him. 'What's going on here has nothing to do with then, and if I'd wanted to get revenge, which I don't, I'd have done it a long time ago.'

'Right. Lincoln Masters and Naxos Capital Assets.' She looked at him shrewdly for a moment before nodding. 'All right. Fair enough. I did think it was a bit of a stretch. I mean, twenty years would be insanely long to bear a grudge.'

Not in his opinion. Not when it fuelled his drive to succeed, his abhorrence of drama and his determination to avoid commitment at all costs. 'And let's not forget,' he said, refusing to consider for even a second that she might have a point, '*you* seduced *me*.'

'Does that happen often?'

'Never.'

'No wonder you were so angry and ran away in such a hurry.'

'I did not run away,' he said with a grind of his teeth. 'I simply don't like losing control.' His jaw clenched tighter when a faint smile curved her gorgeous mouth. 'What's so amusing?'

'You must admit there's a certain symmetry to

it.' An unsettling glint lit the dark brown depths of her eyes. 'I mean, your father and my mother, then you and me, all this time later.'

'It's not the same thing at all,' he said, a cold sweat breaking out at the thought of being sucked into her orbit, swallowed up and spat out when she was done with him. 'What happened between us was strictly a one-off.'

'Why? I agree that there are a lot of unknowns about this whole arrangement, but you know as well as I do that the sex would be great. I mean, the way things ended notwithstanding, that encounter in Switzerland was scorching. And we still share an uncommonly intense attraction. It was there yesterday and it's here now. So why fight it? Are you a fan of celibacy? I'm not.'

Well, no, of course he wasn't. But lust had got him into this mess in the first place and he was never succumbing to it again. Prioritising their child and avoiding screwing it up through reckless and selfish indulgence was the whole bloody point of this. He would fight the attraction—that unfortunately he couldn't deny—until his dying breath.

So his body, which was all for closing the space between them and spreading her out on the island, could forget it. And Olympia should abandon any designs she might have on him too. Perhaps she assumed she could wrap him around her little finger, as no doubt she had with countless other men, but if she did, she was dead wrong. She might be as dangerously beautiful as Helen of Troy and as doggedly persistent as Genghis Khan, but he wasn't a toy to be played with or a land to be conquered. And she was obviously used to being indulged and getting her own way, but not this time and not by him. He'd built an empire out of nothing. He'd overcome bigger hurdles and faced down tougher opponents than her. He would not be swayed. He would never yield to her allure, no matter how loudly the voice in his head demanded it. He would never be that weak.

'Further complicating an already complicated situation is a terrible idea,' he said in a tone that even he could hear brooked no argument. 'We owe it to our child to stay focused. To give it one hundred per cent. So there will be no sex. Either now or in the future. And that's final.'

CHAPTER SEVEN

OLYMPIA FOUND THE knowledge that the affair between their parents remained in the past reassuring. Not only would it make the future tricky if Alex still had a problem with her mother—who had a tendency to pop up unexpectedly—but also she did not appreciate the thought of being manipulated and used for revenge.

Other elements of their conversation, however, gave her grave cause for concern. What gave him the right to bulldoze her perfectly valid observations about their relationship? she thought, as they monosyllabically munched their way through a lunch of prawns, olives, tomatoes and bread, which his housekeeper had laid out beneath the vine-heavy pergola that covered the terrace. Who'd made him the boss of this? Confidence was one thing, but arrogance and presumption were something else entirely.

She was developing the impression that he actively wanted to make their arrangement as difficult as possible, although for the life of her she couldn't work out why that would be. It didn't seem at all complicated to her. As they'd already established, they had seven months before the baby put in an appearance. There was plenty of time to indulge the attraction before having to switch their attention elsewhere.

So maybe *everything* was a battle for control. Maybe he got a kick out of catching her on the back foot. Or maybe he was simply a masochist. Who knew? One thing she *did* know was that having him eating out of her hand clearly wasn't going to be as easy as she'd assumed, which was not only irritating but also alarming, because she liked being liked. It made her feel good about herself. When people did what she wanted, her self-esteem rocketed.

Conversely, rejection, which she'd always hated, invariably triggered a painful sense of unattractiveness and invalidation. In the past, this had brought about some pretty self-destructive behaviour. One night, after a few too many tequila shots as a result of being ghosted by a guy she'd briefly hooked up with, she'd danced naked in the fountain at Trafalgar Square, which had led to an embarrassing brush with the police, a one thousand pound fine and headlines the next morning that had not been kind.

It was obvious that Alex didn't like her. He clearly found her aggravating and considered her manipulative. He didn't trust her not to mess this parenting business up and he had no respect for the effort she was trying to make with regard to her career. In fact, his opinion of her could not be any lower and that was worrying. Despite his apparent commitment to their baby, her situation felt precarious. What if she did something that made him back out of their marriage of convenience? What if he decided she was too much to take on—or too little, for that matter—and realised he could provide just as well for their child without having to be involved with her?

She couldn't allow that. She needed his protection, and therefore she had to mitigate the risk of him disappearing and bind him to her and the baby a little more tightly for both their sakes. Perhaps she should seduce him again. Bamboozle him with sex. That might raise her in his estimation. He was adamant that it wasn't happening, yet their chemistry was still off the charts. It would strengthen their connection. The boost to her self-esteem would be just what she needed. So what if she took to floating about the place in nothing but a skimpy pair of bikini bottoms and asking him at intervals to rub sunscreen into her back? She reckoned he would last five minutes tops with her stretching and purring beneath his hands.

And what if she combined that plan with something else? Like, say, a party to celebrate their engagement with family and friends. Wouldn't that double down on achieving the security she was after? Marriage would be harder to get out of once they'd announced it to the world, surely. And quite apart from that, it would have myriad other benefits, benefits that were crashing through her thoughts even now.

'Alex?' she said, so convinced by the rightness of her inspired idea that she couldn't keep it to herself.

'Mmm?'

'I think we should throw an engagement party.'

In response to this bald announcement, which sounded oddly loud after such a long period of silence, Alex's head shot up and his brow furrowed. 'An engagement party?' he echoed, evidently not as enamoured of the idea as she was, if his look of horror was anything to go by.

'Yes,' she said, her brain already beginning to ping with ideas. 'Nothing big. Just a couple of hundred or thereabouts. Food. A DJ. That sort of thing. We could have it here. In the garden. Lights in the pool. In the trees. It would be quite the event.'

'Absolutely not.'

'Why not?'

He sat back and stared at her as if she'd sprouted horns. 'What on earth makes you think an engagement party is necessary? I hope you haven't forgotten already that nothing about our arrangement is real.'

Something twanged in her chest at that, but she ignored it. 'Don't worry,' she said firmly, although she wasn't entirely sure which of them she was trying to convince most. 'I haven't forgotten anything, and I am well aware that nothing about this is real.' Which was fine, of course. Because that had been the plan all along and would continue to be. 'However, there are a number of reasons why it's an excellent idea.'

'Such as?'

'Well, firstly, it would be a good opportunity for you to meet my family. Some of my siblings are around in the next couple of weeks. You could rekindle your relationship with Leo. Meet the others. It has to be done some time. My mother wouldn't be in attendance if that's what's worrying you,' she assured him when she saw that he'd gone a little pale. 'She's been in Argentina for the last month and, as far as I understand, is planning on staying there for the foreseeable future. On an estancia with a cattle billionaire. The best place for her, if you ask me. Nice and far away. Furthermore, it would be an opportunity to fix the mess you made by pre-empting our news. I could use the occasion to spin the idea that I've moved on from my past. From what Leo said, it doesn't sound as though you provided much in the way of detail about what's going on, so why couldn't we have reached a deeper understanding in the interim? It's a win-win on a number of levels, don't you agree?'

Olympia sat back, rather pleased with the robustness of her argument, until Alex leaned forward and gave his head a sharp shake. 'I couldn't agree less,' he said flatly. 'It's a no-win on every level. And none of it is happening.'

She blinked at the harshness of his tone. 'Why not?'

'I don't do parties.'

'That's not a problem. I do parties enough for the both of us. I excel at putting on a show. All you'd have to do is turn up.'

'No.'

'Don't you think you owe me?'

'I don't owe you anything,' he said, a muscle ticking in his jaw. 'I've already apologised for speaking to Leo. We're not throwing a party.'

Agh. Why was he such a control freak? 'Well, *I* might.'

'With the groom nowhere to be seen? Wouldn't that negate the object of the exercise? I'd think twice if I were you.'

He was right, dammit. It would totally negate the object of the exercise. 'Is there anything I can do to persuade you otherwise?'

'Not a thing. Now, you'll have to excuse me,' he said, giving her a wintry smile as he pushed his chair back and got to his feet. 'I have work to do.'

Given that he'd spent pretty much the entire afternoon in his study sitting at his desk, Alex had achieved precious little. On a Saturday, the markets were closed but there was still a tonne of research and analysis to do before they reopened first thing on Monday morning. He had meetings to prepare for. Investment strategies to define.

However, he'd been so unsettled by the events of today that he hadn't been able to concentrate. Reports lay untouched and files remained unread. In fact, it was a good thing he hadn't been able to trade because, if he had, he might well have made a careless mistake and lost millions. He was that distracted.

As if the morning hadn't been enough of an upheaval, he'd had to contend with lunch. He'd spent the first half of it dwelling on everything Olympia had flung at him in the kitchen. Quite apart from the irritating defiance she'd displayed and the fact that she was totally unintimidated by him, which, he was prepared to admit, piqued his vanity, he'd never met anyone so unafraid to voice the thoughts in their head. To so boldly and unashamedly state what they wanted and go for it. At least, not on a personal level, and he found it as confusing as hell. One minute she was seducing him in stairwells and planning to manipulate the truth for her own purposes—which indicated he shouldn't trust her—and the next she was unguardedly and transparently detailing her vulnerabilities and her desires—which suggested he could.

Which was the real her?

What should he believe?

He couldn't work it out.

Then she'd hit him with the engagement party. Where that idea had sprung from he had no clue, but he should have guessed she'd do something at some point to wreck his illusion of control because it happened all too often. Nothing big? Two hundred people? And to think he'd imagined she sometimes felt as lonely as he did. He must have lost his mind.

Quite honestly, there was nothing he'd rather do less than attend a party filled with Stanhopes. By managing his attendance at both corporate and social events, he'd succeeded in avoiding most of them these last twenty years. The thought of being confronted by a handful at once, and the memories he'd subsequently be battered with, made his brain bleed, which was why he'd put his foot down.

Besides, who would he invite to such a thing? Unlike her, he had no family and few friends. No doubt if he'd agreed she'd have pressed him for a guest list, which he wouldn't have been able to provide, and that would have led to questions about his past and how he felt about it that he never wanted to answer.

Such discombobulation had been behind his decision to hole up here until he got it all straight, not that he'd had any success. His brain simply refused to function. He was too wound up.

And then, a couple of hours ago, Olympia had

pitched up at the pool, and soon after that he'd given up all pretence of work. When she'd removed her robe to reveal the stunning body beneath he'd nearly swallowed his tongue. Her gold bikini was barely there. Just four small triangles held together with what looked like string. Her limbs were long and toned, her curves spectacular, her stomach still flat, and in the light of the afternoon sun she seemed to glow.

All thoughts of parties and meetings and clients and IPOs had flown from his head. Transfixed, he'd watched her dive neatly into the water and had been walloped by the urge to join her. When she'd finished her swim, she'd dried off and then had twisted herself into a series of poses that might have been yogic, but definitely made him think of other situations where such flexibility might be a benefit.

Before settling down to sunbathe, she'd applied sunscreen and his fingers had itched to do it for her. He already knew the shape of her breasts and the softness of her skin, but his memory was sketchy. He wanted to reacquaint himself with those parts of her he'd once touched, and explore the rest. At length and with great thoroughness. He wanted to taste her again so badly that his mouth actually watered.

And now, as she stirred from what had looked like a nap and rose from the sun lounger to take another dip, he was wondering, suddenly, why shouldn't he?

Why was he denying himself that pleasure when he didn't have to? He was soon to marry a confusing woman who caused him all kinds of grief, but to whom he was also insanely attracted, and he'd committed himself to a lifetime of celibacy because there was no way in hell *he* would break his marriage vows, even if they were merely a technicality.

What on earth had he been thinking? Why had he done that? Because he feared the desire he felt for her getting out of hand and somehow destroying him? It wouldn't. If anything, it would lessen. It always did. Most likely it would burn out within days and settle into something entirely manageable. So this relationship didn't have to be a crazed, lust-filled nightmare. Nor did it have to be sexless. And God, it would be novel to engage with her in an activity that he did understand.

Olympia emerged from the pool, a fluid movement of undulating curves, the water sluicing over her like a caress, and barely before he was aware of what he was doing, Alex was throwing his glasses onto his desk, leaping out of his chair and striding out of the study, across the hall and into the sitting room. He pushed open the French doors and stepped out onto the terrace, every cell of his body rigid with tension, his pulse hammering so hard he could hear it in his ears.

All he could think about as he stalked towards her was hauling her into his arms, crushing his mouth to hers and losing himself in the dynamite heat they generated together. The scent and taste of her had kept him awake all that night in Switzerland. Back in his suite, he'd lost count of the number of times he'd nearly caved in and stormed to her room to find out exactly what they could do in a bed.

Well, now was his chance.

When Olympia saw Alex bearing down on her like a thunderstorm, her heart gave a great lurch and then began to race. She'd been poolside for two hours now, and she'd been bordering on desperate, but now it looked as though Plan B might be working.

With his intransigence over the party, the only option he'd left her with to secure his commitment was seduction. To that end, having recalled from the morning's tour that his desk overlooked the pool, she'd decided on a swim. She'd been feeling hot and prickly anyway, but if he happened to spot her scantily clad body out of the study window, and found himself suddenly so helpless to resist the attraction he'd all but admitted he still felt that he ravished her on a sun lounger, wouldn't that represent the win she was after? Wouldn't she be strengthening his connection to their baby through her? And on a more personal level, wouldn't the collapse of his resistance and his surrender to temptation be empowering and satisfying and brilliant? As she'd stripped off her sundress and donned her bikini, Olympia had rather thought it would.

She hadn't expected it to take this long. His will-power was formidable indeed. But judging by the way his dark-as-night eyes were locked onto hers and the determination with which his jaw was set, it looked as though her bikini, yoga, sunscreen ruse might have worked. He was focusing on her so intently that she was rooted to the spot. He radiated such predatory intensity that she'd never felt so vindicated. Or so palpably excited. But she would be wise to exercise caution. He could be out here for any number of reasons, and he had a habit of behaving in ways she did not anticipate, so she wouldn't be taking anything for granted. He came to an abrupt stop a couple of feet in front of her and it was all she could do to carry on squeezing the water from her hair and stay where she was.

'What's happened?' she asked, trying to suppress the adrenaline that was flooding her system as hot thrills of anticipation shot down her spine. 'Is something wrong?'

His laser-like gaze roamed over her so slowly and thoroughly that it left a trail of fire across her skin and a muscle began to hammer in his jaw. 'Nothing's happened and there's nothing wrong,' he said, his voice edged with a roughness that made him sound as though he'd swallowed a bucket of gravel.

'You look a little unhinged,' she said, her nerve-endings quivering madly in response.

'I feel a little unhinged.'

'Then what is it?'

'It's you.'

Her heart almost stopped. Could this plan have succeeded where the party suggestion had failed? 'Me?'

His gaze landed on her mouth and darkened. 'I want you,' he practically growled while she thought, *Oh, thank God for that. It's worked.* 'I want to kiss you until neither of us can think straight. Then I intend to carry you up to my bed and keep you there for the next twenty-four hours. After that, we'll see. But as I recall you have two weeks off. I'm sure we can think of interesting ways to fill them.'

Olympia was sure they could. She'd spent the entire afternoon imagining exactly how the immediate future would play out if she had her way. 'What happened to sex complicating things?' she asked, as breathless as if she'd just run the two hundred metres. 'To what we did being a one-off? You were so resolute.'

'I've had a rethink. Sex isn't complicated. It's simply the physical representation of chemistry. It occurred to me that this marriage of ours will likely last years, and in actual fact I'm *not* a fan of celibacy. We're in it for the long haul, and as you pointed out only this morning, we need to make the best of it.'

'I'm delighted we're finally on the same page.'

'Not half as delighted as I am.'

'Then what are you waiting for?'

'I have absolutely no idea.'

With one quick move, he reached out and pulled her into his arms. As his mouth crashed down on hers, Olympia threw her arms around his neck and sank into his powerful embrace. She closed her eyes and gave herself up to a sizzling kiss that lit a bonfire of desire inside her and instantly transported her to a plane where nothing existed but oblivion. His hands roamed over her back before settling, one between her shoulder blades, the other on her bottom, and he didn't need to pull her in because she was already plastered up against him, as close as she could get.

He was big and hard everywhere, which made her feel unbelievably soft and delicate, and she must be soaking him through but that didn't appear to bother him. All he seemed to care about as he lowered her to a sun lounger and eased her back—his body blotting out the sun so completely that all she could see was him—was getting her horizontal.

And why would she complain about that when the feel of his weight pressing down on her was so delicious? Why would she complain about anything when she was enveloped in such scorching heat and the rigidly controlled strength that she couldn't wait to unleash? When she felt so blisteringly fabulous?

She knew that the euphoria would fade once they'd satisfied their desire. It always did and always too soon. But the great thing about this particular situation was that she could just have another hit whenever she needed one. She could have this every day of the week if she wanted, because she would do her best to ensure that he was going nowhere.

And anyway, why was she even thinking about what happened next? Why was she thinking at all? Shouldn't her brain be in bits? Shouldn't she be focusing on getting him as naked as he was trying to get her?

Why was she suddenly bothering about whether or not she might have coerced him into this, and what was that thing that had been niggling away at the back of her mind all afternoon and was now screeching through her thoughts like a claxon? Why couldn't she shake it?

It was something else she'd learned in rehab, she realised with a jolt as he wrenched his mouth from hers, dragging it down her neck to rain kisses along the slope of her right breast while one hand caressed her left, the other making quick work of the knot that held her bikini top in place. Something she'd completely forgotten about because, up until the mad half an hour with him in Switzerland, she'd been too focused on work for it to come up, and afterwards she'd been too wrapped up in rejection and shame to see it.

Her use of sex as a coping mechanism.

As a way of getting attention and feeling valued.

Of temporarily blocking the constant turmoil with which she lived, replacing it with a few blissful hours of wild abandon—her standard operating procedure for years.

She'd done it that night back in May, provoking him into giving her what she'd wanted because she equated sexual acceptance to personal acceptance, and she was doing it again. Right now. Not only had she engineered him into this, to secure his commitment and to make herself feel good, and a little less lonely, but she was also trying to change the way he felt about her, to get him to like her. And if she let this reach its natural conclusion it could mean undoing all the hard work she'd put into trying to understand that her value wasn't tied up in sex and other people. That it had to come from a solid sense of self and emotional independence, rather than an unreliable and unpredictable external source. Much of the progress she'd made would be gone, just like that.

So she had to put a stop to it, she thought dazedly, fighting for control even though she still shook with desire and her body screamed in protest. She had to reset the boundaries and continue to put the effort in now, for the sake of her future self. She didn't want to go back to the person she'd been before.

She wanted to look and move forward. And she could not afford to jeopardise the precious new life she was carrying by careering down that slippery slope. So thank God she'd had this epiphany before it was too late.

Digging deep to silence the voice in her head insisting it didn't have to be this way—didn't she *need* to lock him in? Didn't she *want* to feel good?— Olympia opened her eyes and blinked away the fog. While she still had the ability to resist him, she summoned up every drop of physical and emotional strength she possessed.

She put her hands on his shoulders, gave him a little push, and panted, 'Stop, Alex. Stop.'

CHAPTER EIGHT

ALEX MIGHT HAVE been so addled with need that he'd
lost his mind along with his control, but he wasn't
so far gone that Olympia's tremulous but firm plea
didn't pierce the haze in his brain. It did. And the
second it did, his blood chilled and he froze. He
jerked his head up as if she'd slapped him, shock ric-
ocheting through him, his breathing fast and harsh.

'What's wrong?' he grated, scouring her face
for some sort of clue as to what was going on. He
couldn't read her expression, but the fierce heat had
faded from her gaze, he just about managed to note.
The pressure of her hands on his shoulders was light
but firm. Unmistakable evidence that she was not as
into this as he was. But she had been. He was sure
of it. So what had changed?

'We need to stop.'

'Yes, I got that,' he said, perhaps a little sharply,
but then he was confused, in physical pain and being
battered by the concern that he was somehow at
fault. 'But why? Is it the baby?'

'What? No. It's not the baby.' A faint frown creased

her forehead. 'It's just that you're not the only one who's had a rethink.'

She pushed at him again, and with Herculean effort and a whole lot of discomfort, he lifted himself off her. Somehow, he made it to the sun lounger next to hers, watching uncomprehendingly as she picked up her robe and pulled it on. When she drew the sides together and tied the belt around her waist, hiding from sight the luscious body he'd planned to reacquaint himself with over the next two weeks, the disappointment that seared through him was like a punch to the gut. 'I don't understand.'

'I've changed my mind,' she said. 'You're right. Celibacy *is* the way forward. Maybe not for ever, but certainly for the time being.'

Denial careened through him fast and hard. Hadn't they dealt with this? 'It absolutely is *not* the way forward.'

'It is for me.'

'Why?'

'Because I can't engage in casual sex right now. Or any sex for that matter. It's not good for my recovery.'

He stilled and stared at her in bewilderment. What was she talking about? The sex, more intense and satisfying than any he'd ever known, and potentially continuing for years, would be anything but casual. And recovery? From what? 'What do you mean?'

LUCY KING   109

'As I'm sure you're aware, not so long ago I spent three months in rehab.'

Somehow he managed to nod. He'd read about it in the press at the time. But... 'What does that have to do with this?'

'While I was there I underwent a lot of therapy, which, among many other things, taught me that I use sex as a coping mechanism. To make myself feel less empty and not quite so rubbish about myself. Not all that often,' she was quick to add. 'I wasn't nearly as promiscuous as the press made out. But enough for it to be a problem. And it never worked because the satisfaction was always fleeting. After the initial high wore off I would inevitably be back at square one.'

He frowned, shoved his hands through his hair and then rubbed them over his face, trying to compute what she was telling him, an almost impossible task right now. 'Is that what happened in Switzerland?' he asked, feeling slightly sick at the thought that sex with him might have had such an effect.

'Yes,' she confirmed, and his stomach turned harder, even though by deploying the few brain cells that were still functioning he could just about understand on an intellectual level that it wasn't him per se, although the way he'd dashed off that night couldn't have helped. 'You were right when you said that shouldn't have happened. It really shouldn't. I'd been so focused on work that I somehow managed to forget everything I learned on that front. And then afterwards, ironically, I was too preoccupied with the way it had made me feel to think about why. I only remembered it just now.'

'Your timing is terrible.'

'I know. I'm sorry. But I can't make the same mistake again. I need to break the habit and find my self-worth elsewhere. And that means steering clear of sex until I can value myself for being me. I apologise for giving you a different impression. I shouldn't have led you on. I'm a work in progress.'

'You didn't lead me on,' he said, thinking that it had been his decision to overturn his vow that there would be no sex in this relationship, no one else's. She hadn't forced him to abandon work and come out here. He'd done that totally voluntarily.

'I don't normally do yoga at the pool. That was purely for your benefit. It's clear you neither like me nor approve of me and I was feeling a little insecure about your commitment to our baby. I thought I could strengthen it with the party, and when that didn't work, through sex. But I shouldn't have done it. It was manipulative of me and wrong and I apologise for that too.'

Right.

God.

What was it about this woman that turned him into such an unsuspecting fool?

'You have no reason to doubt my commitment,'

he said, sweating at the thought of how easily he'd been seduced once again. 'Thanks to your mother, I've witnessed first-hand the devastation the breakdown of a family can wreak, and there is no way on earth I would allow any child of mine to suffer like that. So we're in this together until he or she can fend for itself.'

'What happened?'

'It's not important.'

'I'd like to understand.'

'Yes, well, I'd like a cold shower.'

'Of course,' she said, reddening. 'I'm sorry.'

And now, unfathomably, he was the one to feel like a heel. 'Whatever your reasons for starting this, you never need to apologise for changing your mind.'

'Are you sure?'

'Quite sure,' he confirmed because, on that point at least, he was. What he was going to do about the crucifying sexual frustration, the continuing befuddlement and the frighteningly weak defences he had against her, however, he had no idea. Removing himself from her unsettling orbit seemed like a good place to start, so he got to his feet, gave her a nod and said, before turning on his heel and heading back into the house, 'Enjoy the rest of your afternoon.'

The relief that Olympia felt at Alex listening to and respecting her position on the subject of sex was immense. She hadn't been sure how he'd react. Other men of her acquaintance might not have been quite so accommodating, although to be fair she'd never put a stop to proceedings before so she couldn't say for sure. She felt that he, on the other hand, really was a man of strength and integrity and tolerance, because his disappointment had been obvious. And to take her confession that she'd been out to seduce him so lightly, well, that had been a relief too, although unexpected. But perhaps he appreciated her candidness.

However, over the course of the following day it became apparent that he was not handling the situation as well as she'd assumed. Her attempts at conversation were met with increasingly terse replies. Her enquiries into what effect her mother's affair with his father had had on him, something she just couldn't seem to let go, were stonewalled entirely. Eye contact deteriorated and he kept vanishing into his study.

On Monday morning she woke to an empty house and the petrifying thought that she'd pushed him too far. That—thanks to her bid to satisfy her insatiable curiosity about his past and her crippling insecurities, which meant she was now the one blowing hot and cold—he'd finally had enough.

Her heart thudded loudly in the eerie silence as she searched for him in vain. Where could he have gone? Had he been in such a hurry he couldn't even leave a note? What did that mean for her and the baby?

Back in the kitchen, but feeling too sick for breakfast, she brought up his number on her phone. Not altogether surprisingly, the call went to voicemail. So she sent him a text, and after thirty agonising minutes of pacing up and down, wondering whether she'd blown things for good with her reckless impulsivity and persistence, her phone pinged with a reply.

He was at the office. Apparently, because of a truncated Friday afternoon and disrupted weekend, he'd had a mountain of work to get through before the markets had opened this morning. He wasn't sure when he'd be back. Tuesday, perhaps, or Wednesday. He would mostly likely be uncontactable for much of the time, but his housekeeper was on hand for anything she required.

That all sounded very much like an excuse, Olympia thought, her hands shaking a little as she filled a glass with water. He'd spent much of the weekend holed up in his study here, precisely for the purpose of catching up. And Athens wasn't so far it necessitated an overnight stay. He was avoiding her. That much was obvious. Because he was having second thoughts? Or could he be after a woman who wouldn't lead him on and then change her mind? None of that bore thinking about.

So what was she going to do?

Well, she could follow him into the city and demand to know what he was playing at, which was what her instincts were urging her to do. On the other hand, the more circumspect voice in her head—which sounded a lot like one of her therapists in rehab—insisted that she might be wise to exercise caution. Patience wasn't something she'd ever been particularly good at, but look at where a lack of it had got her. Fretting and stressing and potentially abandoned. Applying more pressure to an already fragile situation could turn out to be a terrible idea. She couldn't blame him if he needed some time to get his head around everything that had happened recently. She did too. It had been pretty intense. Hard to be believe it had been only three days, really. And she knew she was a handful.

So as much as it went against her natural inclination to track him down, she would give him the space he needed and trust that he wasn't wrapped around some uncomplicated woman who he didn't dislike. She'd keep herself occupied for the next day or two—somehow—and if he hadn't reappeared by the middle of the week, she'd reassess. She'd use the time to revisit everything she'd learned in rehab with a view to the future. She'd call her brother and see if he had any insight into the impact of the affair. She'd turn her thoughts to how she'd like to raise her baby, and consider the extent to which her mother was, in fact, going to be a problem. She'd take it easy and refuse to catastrophise.

It was thirty-six hours max, she told herself, concentrating on breathing slowly and deeply until the panic subsided. Not long at all. How hard could it be?

Despite innumerable cold showers and many frustratingly futile hours locked away in his study, by Sunday night Alex had known that he couldn't stick around at the villa any longer.

To his intense frustration, he was unable to get his response to Olympia under control. His dreams were filled with alternative endings to Saturday afternoon by the pool, visions that had her not pushing him away but pulling him in. Fielding her increasingly probing questions had become so stressful that his muscles ached with tension.

His nerves were fraying. The constant wariness and the unassuaged desire made him feel tense and on edge. He had tried to keep his distance, but she'd drawn him like a magnet nonetheless. The air had seemed to be filled with her scent. He'd been aware of her even when he couldn't see her.

And, as if managing that wasn't enough of a challenge, he couldn't get to grips with various aspects of her personality and his inability to read any of them. She tied him in knots, which no one had ever done before. It was draining and bewildering.

His self-control had never felt so under threat. He hadn't liked any of it, which was why he'd got up at the crack of dawn, having barely slept a wink anyway, and driven back to Athens. But he might as well not have bothered because, by late Tuesday afternoon, restlessness was kicking in and his conscience was giving him grief. He'd worked precisely nothing out and he still dreamed of her, he was still obsessing over the questions she'd thrown at him, so what had been the purpose of escape? Didn't avoiding her like this smack of cowardice? And what was he planning to do? Stay out of her way for ever? Well, that wasn't going to work. At some point he was going to have to face her again and he'd never been one to procrastinate.

He had to get over himself, he thought grimly as he snatched up his phone and keys and stalked out of the office because staying here in the city was no longer feasible. He had no choice. He couldn't keep dashing off whenever she hurled him off balance. Where would that leave their child? He had to make his relationship with Olympia work, and he'd come to the conclusion that the only way to achieve that was to find out what made her tick. Only by knowing her would he understand her, and only by understanding her would he be able to anticipate her moves and regain control.

Of course, by embarking on such an enterprise he'd probably end up learning far more about the Stanhopes than he'd ever be comfortable with. Containing how he felt about her mother might be tricky.

But it wasn't as if he'd be sucked into any sort of emotional connection with her, and he was in a permanent state of discomfort anyway. If push came to shove he could answer any questions she may have about him with the baldest of facts. He needn't disclose anything of importance. They needn't discuss him at all. This course of action would be one hundred per cent about her. He would unravel her secrets if it was the last thing he did. He wasn't used to failing and he wouldn't in this.

By Tuesday evening, Olympia was practically climbing the walls. She'd discovered that patience was far harder to implement than she'd anticipated. There was only so much taking it easy she could stand. Leo had had no insight into anything. Within hours she'd been itching to hop in the car and drive to Alex's office to demand to know what was going on.

However, by drumming up the strategies she'd learned in rehab to curb her impulses, she'd resisted. She'd swum so many lengths of the pool she could practically have reached Crete. Every time her thoughts turned to what he was getting up to and who with, or what he might be planning, she closed her eyes and practised the mindfulness that would stop them spinning out of control. No good would come of second-guessing his intentions. Confronting him in person could make matters worse. All she could do was wait. For a little while longer, at least.

But it hadn't been easy. Her nerves were stretched to their absolute limit. And, when she heard the slam of the front door, shattering the silence, the tension drained from her body so fast she went dizzy.

God, it was good to see him, she thought when a few moments later he appeared on the terrace, where she sat trying to concentrate on a book while the sun set in front of her. He looked so handsome in a dark suit and white shirt, which was unbuttoned at the top to reveal a tantalising wedge of chest. A light stubble covered his jaw and his hair was dishevelled as if he'd been ploughing his hands through it.

And she'd missed him, she was surprised to realise. Which was ridiculous when she'd only moved in five days ago, but what a rollercoaster of a ride those five days had been. The first three had been so energising and thrilling—the last two so flat and dull.

However, how he looked and how she felt about it was irrelevant. All that mattered was that he'd returned. And from now on, she vowed, she would do her level best not to rock the boat further. She would shove a lid on her insecurities and bury the attraction that hadn't diminished one bit. She'd draw a line under everything that had happened to date and start again. She'd be cool and composed, as compliant as she could manage, and channel the mature, responsible adult she was trying to become. The security of her baby depended on it.

'You're back,' she said, reduced to stating the obvious from the sheer relief that perhaps she hadn't screwed up after all. 'How was the city?'

'Busy,' he said, as he pulled out a chair and sat down opposite her.

'Did you get done what you needed to get done?'

'In a manner of speaking.'

'What does that mean?'

'We need to talk.'

At that, Olympia stilled. Her heart plummeted and she briefly thought she might throw up, because that was a phrase no one ever wanted to hear. But she swallowed down the flare of panic that threatened her control, and she fought back the urge to throw herself at him and beg for forgiveness. 'I apologise for my behaviour on Saturday,' she said, just about managing to keep her emotions contained. 'I'll endeavour to do better in future. You have my word.'

His eyebrows rose. 'Do I?'

'Absolutely.'

'Good to know.' He sat back and studied her for a moment with his dark glittering gaze, as if the self-doubt she was riddled with was written all over her face. 'I thought we could start with you.'

She stared at him blankly. 'What?'

'I'm interested in hearing more about those family dynamics you mentioned.'

Her heart skipped a beat. Now *her* eyebrows were the ones to shoot up. 'You actually want to talk?'

'Yes. That's what I said.' He frowned. 'Why? What did you think I meant?'

'Nothing,' she said, getting a grip and silently cursing the low self-esteem that made her immediately imagine the worst. 'Ignore me. Pregnancy hormones making me a little loopy, that's all. I just feared you might have given me up as a lost cause, that's all.'

'I would never abandon my child.'

She flushed. 'No, of course not.'

'And talking was your idea in the first place, as I recall.' He sat back and stretched out his legs. 'So shoot.'

'Now?'

'You advocated getting a move on.'

Yes, she'd done that too. So why was she hesitating? Nothing about her life to date was a secret, and she still believed that them getting to know each other was the best chance their relationship had of success. Once she'd answered his questions, he could finally answer hers, and they could move forward. There was no cause for concern.

'Right,' she said, reminding herself that she'd been through it a dozen times in therapy and this would be no different. 'Well. As you must know, I'm the youngest of six. Leo's ten years older than me. Zander, Thalia, Atticus and Daphne are in between. Our parents weren't exactly what you might call nurturing. To be honest, they were so negligent that, if they hadn't had money and status, they'd probably have been in jail. My mother is selfishness personified and my father was the stiff-upper-lip type who believed that children should be seen and not heard. Apart from Leo, of course, who he was grooming to take over the family business. The rest of us were mainly brought up by nannies.'

'That must have been difficult.'

'I didn't know any different at the time,' she said with a shrug that belied just how traumatic it had been. 'And materially we wanted for nothing, of course, so I'm aware I'm playing the world's tiniest violin. Nevertheless, as the baby of the family, I got virtually no attention from anyone. I was always overshadowed by my older siblings. I could never work out where I fitted in. None of my accomplishments were original. Things like learning to ride a bike or swim—the others had done it all before. No one was ever impressed by anything I did. Or even vaguely interested. I was virtually invisible.'

'I find that hard to believe,' he murmured, running his gaze slowly over her before returning it to hers.

She ignored the flush of heat his perusal had provoked and forced herself to concentrate. 'Nevertheless, it's true.'

'You don't lack attention now.'

'No, well, I've devoted a lot of time and effort to getting it.'

'How?'

'It's not a pretty story,' she said with a wince.

'Let me be the judge of that.'

But that was what she feared. Him sizing her up and finding her lacking. It was bad enough when people she didn't know did it, but how would she handle the father of her child, her husband-to-be, thinking her even more shallow and pointless than he already did? 'Why don't we talk about your upbringing instead?'

'Because mine wasn't very interesting.'

'I doubt that very much,' she said, her curiosity piqued by the metaphorical doors slamming shut around him. 'You implied that my mother caused the breakdown of your family. What happened? I'd like to know.'

'Maybe later,' he said vaguely. 'Right now, however, I'd like to know more about *you*.'

Her heart gave a little jump, but she managed to keep it under control. 'For the baby's sake.'

He shook his head. 'For my sake. I can't work you out. You repeatedly confound me. It's been driving me mad. That's why I left. And why I've come back. To find out what makes you tick.'

This time, her control was no match for her emotions. This attention he was paying her was for her. Not for the baby, but for her. She'd had so little of it in her life, how could she possibly resist telling him everything he wanted to know? She might never get another chance to be the sole object of his focus, and the need to string it out for as long as possible drummed hard and fast inside her.

'I guess we do have to be open and honest with each other if we're going to make a success of this,' she said, her chest so tight it was making her dizzy.

'Exactly.'

'And you'll keep an open mind?'

'Yes.'

All right, then. She drew in a couple of deep steady breaths to ease the pressure on her lungs and braced herself. 'I must have realised at quite an early age that if I didn't want to disappear entirely I'd have to make myself visible, so I started acting up.'

'In what way?'

'The usual look-at-me things,' she said, recalling fragments of behaviour that had begun innocently enough but had become increasing self-destructive. 'When I was a kid, I was always putting on shows for anyone who would watch. Plays, musicals, any-thing really. I was the ultimate extrovert. Lots of friends, the leader of the gang, that sort of thing. But that didn't work—my family still more or less ignored me—so as I got older I devoted myself to accomplishments that *were* original.'

'Such as?'

'I began shoplifting. Not for the money, obviously. Not even for the high. I think I wanted someone to catch me, although no one ever did. I skipped school and disappeared for hours. Occasionally the alarm was raised, but by the time I was born the nannies had pretty much given up on discipline altogether so nothing ever came of it.'

'You were pushing against boundaries that weren't even there.'

'Right,' she said, marvelling a little at his perceptiveness. 'I had no one to build me up or set me straight. No one who cared. It was a confusing time. And then it got worse.'

'How?'

'When I was twelve and she was thirteen, Daphne was diagnosed with cancer.'

He frowned. 'I didn't know that.'

'It was kept out of the press. It shook us all up. Even our parents managed to put aside some of their self-interest until she went into remission. And I'm really not proud of this,' she said, swallowing down the hot lump of shame that had lodged in her throat, still crushing after all these years, 'but it occurred to me that if I wanted the attention she'd had I'd have to get ill, which was when I really went off the rails.'

'What happened?'

'I developed a mild eating disorder, and when that didn't achieve the desired result I started drinking and dabbling in drugs. Again nothing too serious. Just enough to blot the pain, I guess, because that seemed to make things better. It made me stop caring quite so much. From then on, I gave up trying to attract the attention of my family and dedicated myself to having fun, something I got very good at indeed.'

'Did no one seriously know what was going on?' Alex asked, his tone even, giving nothing away. 'Not even one of your siblings?'

Olympia shook her head, knowing that they weren't to blame. 'I masked what I was really feeling exceptionally well. But even if they had, it had to be me who wanted to change. That's how I ended up in rehab. One of my friends was hospitalised after an overdose. She was fine but it pulled me up short. I saw how my life might turn out if I didn't do something to fix it, so I checked into the clinic in Arizona, and the rest, as they say, is history.'

Done with her story, she stopped, but Alex seemed to have nothing further to say and a heavy silence fell. She searched his face, unable to tell what he was thinking. But she hoped to God it wasn't appal. Or disgust. She hoped he'd kept that mind open and could understand that, despite its inauspicious beginnings, she was trying to turn her life around.

Because what if he didn't? What if he thought her a complete narcissist like her mother, or believed she presented some sort of danger to their child? Might he try and take it away from her? Could he even do that?

Perhaps she'd made a massive mistake in involving him and agreeing to this marriage. Perhaps she ought to leave and find support elsewhere. Surely *one* of her siblings could give her the help she would need?

But no. She was being ridiculous. That would never happen. Of course he wouldn't take her baby away. This wasn't Victorian England. What was she thinking? What she'd told him was a lot to take in, that was all. She'd needed three months to work it through, and still hadn't fully. He'd had it dumped on him in less than five minutes. It was bound to take time to process.

'So there you go,' she prompted when the silence became too thick to bear. 'That's me and my mad family dynamics. Quite something, right?'

CHAPTER NINE

'QUITE SOMETHING' WAS one way to describe it, Alex reflected darkly as everything Olympia had told him flashed around his head like lightning. He didn't know what he'd expected when he'd asked her to expand on her upbringing. He hadn't given it much thought. But it had turned out to be far more complex than he could ever have envisaged. And so—he was coming to realise—was she.

The press had always made her out to be shallow and flighty and, more often than not, a contempt-ible waste of space. And if he was being brutally honest, that was how he'd seen her too, at least ini-tially. But as the details of her childhood had un-folded, even the most cynical of people would have been disabused of any those assumptions, and that included him.

He was the first to admit he was no expert when it came to siblings, but he excelled in applying logic to a situation and, the more he thought about it, the more he felt that she'd simply reacted to a set of circumstances beyond her control. Her most basic emotional needs had not been met. She'd never had any support. No one had ever cared enough to recognise what was going on and address it. Her parents, her siblings, everyone had failed her, and it was therefore no wonder she'd been so troubled. No wonder her self-esteem was on the floor and she struggled to locate her value. And he now completely understood why she'd wanted to spin the story of their relationship, which meant he would probably have to reconsider the idea of the engagement party she'd proposed.

What did come as a surprise, however, was his reaction to her many and varied revelations. An intense wave of anger, frustration and offence on her behalf was sweeping through him. He wanted to shake her siblings and throttle her mother, and not because of what she'd done to him. He wanted to erase from this world every scathing article the press had ever written about her and fire the people responsible.

Most of all, though, he felt a pressing urge to fix the way she viewed herself. He wasn't sure quite why. He wasn't remotely altruistic and, as much as he wanted her in his bed, her efforts to turn her life around deserved his respect and he would never deliberately try to thwart them by falsely building her up.

Perhaps, then, he had in mind their child and its need for stability. His own mother had been anything but emotionally robust, and she'd become even more fragile after his father's sudden death, which was why he'd had to step up to the plate even though he'd been a little more than a kid himself. He'd witnessed the misery self-doubt could cause and he wouldn't wish it on anyone apart from Selene Stanhope. Their child would certainly benefit from two strong secure parents, so yes, that was most likely it.

'I agree that crazy is one way of looking at it,' he said, not much liking the way Olympia had paled and was biting her lip, as if she feared his verdict, which for some unfathomable reason made him want to hit something hard. 'Through no fault of your own you didn't have it easy, and I can understand how and why you made some unwise choices. But we're all shaped by the past and there's nothing any of us can do to change that.'

'Even you?'

'We're not talking about me.'

'Yet.'

'My point is,' he continued, vowing to keep his past private for as long as he possibly could, 'you can reframe the way you perceive it. What you've been through has made you resilient and tough, a survivor. It shows you're open to new and unconventional experiences. You're adventurous and a risk-taker. You're self-aware. You identified a problem and you took action. Decisively. These things are positives, not negatives, and they come from you. No one else. You.'

By the time he'd finished speaking, Olympia was looking a little shell-shocked, which wasn't far off how he was feeling right now. Where all this was coming from he had no clue, and God knew he was no therapist, but it seemed as though he wasn't done, because apparently he had more observations on the subject that were clamouring to be voiced.

'When you started working for Stanhope's,' he said, having shuffled them into some sort of order, 'I thought your appointment an absurd affront to the industry. I didn't think you'd last five minutes—as you know. But I underestimated you. You've proved yourself to be determined and tenacious. You don't give up. You go for what you want and don't stop until you get it. You take no prisoners. I've witnessed that myself on a number of occasions. Even though I disapprove of you trying to steal my number one client, and I wasn't at all happy about being seduced in a stairwell or by the pool, I can't deny you're impressive. You have charm and charisma in abundance. The way you're turning your failures into success is admirable. You should give yourself more credit, Olympia, and believe in your abilities. Because they're not insignificant. They're not insignificant at all.'

Now he really was done, which was just as well, because if his heart beat any harder it would be in danger of cracking a rib. And if her eyes widened any further they'd likely pop out of her head.

'Do you really think all that?' she said breathlessly, clearly stunned.

'I do,' he replied, because in the end it hadn't been hard to identify her strengths, of which, he'd come to realise as she'd shared the details of her upbringing, there were many. He hadn't had to embellish or invent a thing. He did genuinely believe that she was in possession of every trait he'd described. Objectively, it was nothing less than the truth.

'I don't know what to say.'

No, well, in all honesty, he was just as confused as she was. Not by her this time, which made a change, but by himself, because there was nothing objective about the tightness of his chest and the fire powering through his veins. Or about the other adjectives rattling around his head that described her—magnificent, unique, fascinating. He didn't understand what he was doing or what he was feeling, so the rumble his stomach suddenly gave could not have come at a better time.

'Are you hungry?' he asked as, with some relief, he switched his focus from the insanely complicated to the very simple. 'I am. We should eat.'

Olympia followed Alex into the kitchen in something of a daze. He shrugged off his jacket, hunting down some equipment and ingredients while she struggled to make sense of everything he'd said. Her offer to help with the slicing and dicing of the salad vegetables was declined, which on reflection was a good thing. She'd never chopped a tomato in her life and now, with the way her hands seemed to be trembling, was probably not the time to start.

She didn't much follow the conversation over supper. She answered his questions about Daphne's illness automatically, and elaborated on some of the other things she'd got up to as an out-of-control adolescent, but she was so distracted by his alternative view of her character that she hadn't been able to give him or the conversation her full concentration.

She ate the chicken souvlaki and salad without really tasting it. The elderflower pressé she drank slipped down largely unnoticed. She was fleetingly diverted by the flickering candles that cast dancing shadows across the handsome planes of his face, but within moments she was back in her thoughts, trying to get her head around the value he saw in her.

The process was not an easy one. Worthlessness had been entrenched in her for so long that denial was her default setting. It had never occurred to her to find anything constructive in the chaos that had been her life. She'd only ever focused on the destructive, which had been so impactful, and which for the last decade the headlines had reinforced at every available opportunity.

But now she was being forced to give it some

thought, to fight through the denial and try to consider herself in the light that Alex had shone on her. Was she really everything he'd described? Well, yes, perhaps she was. She *was* determined and tough. Persistent and focused. She only had to look at the last year or so to see that. But even before then she'd thrown herself into every decision she'd made. They might not necessarily have been wise ones, but she'd always had a plan and gone with it. She'd always given everything one hundred per cent. And, as he'd pointed out, she was trying her best to put her failures behind her and seek success.

So maybe he wasn't the only one to underestimate her, she thought, as all the revelations he'd unearthed began pinging around her head and zapping the nuggets of self-doubt that plagued her. She'd underestimated herself, and not just on an emotional level. Because she was a dropout who didn't have a clutch of academic qualifications she'd always thought of herself as somehow lesser than her siblings. Deep down she'd considered herself a loser. But that wasn't necessarily the case. The lack of a certificate or two didn't mean anything. She might not have passed any exams but perhaps the charm and charisma he'd identified made up for that deficiency. A piece of paper certainly wouldn't have helped smash the targets Zander had set.

She had to start believing that her worth lay in herself, in her work and in her plans for the future.

She got a thrill out of her brother telling her she'd done well. When she signed another new client, the high she felt was because of something *she'd* achieved. She was stronger and more confident than she'd imagined. Whatever her motives for seeking a good time, she was fun to be around and a loyal friend. And in the last few days, she'd been called impressive—twice.

It had all been there, she thought a little giddily as a wave of acceptance swept away the last vestiges of denial, and she was filled with a strange sense of calm. She'd just needed a nudge in the right direction to realise it, and Alex—clever man that he was—had given her that nudge. For the first time in her life, she could allow herself to take pride in what she was good at rather than wallow in shame over what she wasn't. She could believe that she didn't have to be defined by the past, and that she did have something to offer the world.

And it was all because of him, she thought, her heart rate picking up as she watched him from across the table. He'd been unexpectedly fierce in his defence of her. He'd seen things in her that no one else ever had. To have someone on her side, in her corner, was such an overwhelming concept that she could barely breathe with the force of it. If he protected and looked out for their child in the same steadfast way, it would never have to question its self-worth. It would never make bad decisions and wind up dancing in fountains. It truly would be blessed.

And so perhaps she should start looking for the positives in her relationship with Alex too. Now they were talking, this marriage had a real chance of success. Now she could accept herself as he saw her, there was no reason to hold back. Nothing was stopping her from taking what she wanted, and right now, with hot heady desire suddenly crashing through her, she wanted him.

Alex was fighting a number of internal battles when he noticed a shift in the air that prickled his senses and sent a rash of goosebumps skittering across his skin.

First, there was his suggestion that Olympia reframe her perception of the past, which had somehow lodged in his head and which, no matter how hard he tried, he couldn't shake off. He didn't know where that insight had originated but it had unhelpfully occurred to him since that he could equally apply it to himself. Which made no sense, because his situation was entirely different. His past hadn't had nearly such an impact on him. Up until his father and her mother had had their affair, his life had been uneventful. He'd lacked for nothing either materially or emotionally. He hadn't had to go off the rails to get attention or push at non-existent boundaries. As an only child he'd been doted on.

And yes, things had irrevocably changed once his family had fallen apart, the comfort that he'd taken for granted evaporating virtually overnight. But while he could easily have descended into a boiling pit of anger and resentment, he hadn't. Instead, he'd channelled how he'd felt into restoring the family's fortunes, and once he'd achieved that he'd devoted himself to chasing the success that would make him invincible. He was more than happy with the way that had turned out, so he couldn't for the life of him work out why he was suddenly dwelling on it.

Then there was the desire that burned as brightly as ever. Olympia looked impossibly sexy in her white strapless dress with her dark shining hair tumbling around her shoulders. As supper progressed, increasingly all he'd wanted to do was realise the dreams that had tormented him these past two nights, even though such a course of action was obviously out of the question.

He'd eaten the chicken that had tasted of nothing with gloomy despondency. How long it would take for her to see what he saw? Presumably, that sort of thing took months of contemplation. If he sourced the very best therapists the world had to offer, might that speed the process up? And what if she never reached the point at which she could bring herself to sleep with him? How would he bear it?

But now, suddenly, the night seemed to be crackling with electricity, as if a storm had enveloped them, and when he glanced up to find her gaze on him—intense, hot, shimmering—every cell of his body stilled. A surge of adrenaline dried his mouth and kickstarted his pulse.

What was going on?

'Why are you looking at me like that?' he asked, his voice thick and strained, even to his own ears.

'Like what?'

'As if you're thinking about kissing me.'

Her gaze dropped to his mouth and darkened and the world seemed to glide to a halt. 'Because I am,' she said with a huskiness that tightened his stomach and sent all his blood straight to his groin. 'And it's not just kissing you that's running through my mind.'

'Oh?'

'I want to finish what I started by the pool.'

Images from that afternoon flashed through his mind. How good she'd felt. How crazed he'd been. Instinct urged him to leap to his feet, grab her by the hand and haul her up the stairs, but his head was yelling *no!* Despite their earlier conversation, he still had little understanding of how she operated. This could be another attempt to manipulate him. Or it might give rise to another about turn when her insecurities took over.

'What's brought this on?' he asked, doing his best to suppress the urgent response of his body because he didn't think he could face another cold shower. 'I thought you were embracing celibacy.'

She shook her head. 'Not any more. And it's you who's brought this on. With all those things you said about me. Your reframing of the past worked. You've made me recognise the value I have and re-alise what I'm capable of.'

He swallowed hard. 'That was quick.'

'I know. But it was all there. I just needed a push in the right direction, which you gave me. If fund management doesn't work out you could make a fortune as a therapist. Mine never even suggested it. I'm very grateful. I'd like to show you exactly how much.'

'Is that right?'

'It couldn't be more right. I know I have many faults, and I know the incident by the pool may suggest otherwise, but prick teasing has never been my thing.' She tilted her head and gave him a smile that, for some reason, struck him square in the chest. 'There's no reason sex can't be just sex, right?'

Well, yes. That was what he'd always believed and a policy he'd always followed. But this would not be the short-term affair he usually favoured. This would be something that would likely tangle him up for years, with an outcome that was any-thing but clear.

On the other hand, it was entirely possible he was overthinking things. He could understand how her

many insecurities might lead to a need for control
that he'd misread as deliberate manipulation. The
real her might well be transparent and honest. Why
shouldn't he trust that it was? And who was he to
question her decision anyway? Hadn't he just pointed
out her capabilities in that area?

He wanted her with a desperation that was turning him inside out and he could see no reason to
deny it. Once the chemistry was addressed the tension between them would vanish. The insatiable
lust he had for her would lessen. And what better
way to distract her whenever she asked him a question he'd rather not have to answer? The benefits of
taking her up on her offer would be many indeed.

'You see,' he said, sitting back, watching her
closely as his blood thickened and his body hard-
ened even more. 'Determined and tenacious. You
go for what you want.'

'I want you.'

'Are you sure?'

'Absolutely.'

'Then come and get me.'

Olympia regarded him for one heart-stopping
moment and then, without taking her eyes off his,
rose from her chair in a move that could only be described as sinuous. His pulse thudded heavily as she
lifted the hem of her dress and slipped off her underwear. Then she sidled over to him and pushed his
legs apart. She dropped to her knees and his temper-

ature rocketed. She unbuckled his belt and tugged down his zip to free him, and when she leaned forward to take him first in her hand and then in her mouth, he nearly passed out with pleasure.

Shuddering, unable to hold back a rough groan, he tangled his hands in her hair and closed his eyes, thinking that if this was the way she showed her gratitude he'd make more of an effort in future to deserve it.

The ministrations of her soft hands and warm wet mouth were sending molten currents through his body, into his head and destroying his brain cells. Tension gripped his muscles, tightening them to the point of pain, and he could feel the need for release swelling fast and hard—but it was too soon. He wanted to demolish her control, as she did his. One part of him, a part he didn't wish to analyse too closely, wanted to make her pay for the torment she'd put him through these past few days.

'Enough,' he grated before he reached the point of no return.

Ignoring her faint mewl of protest, he pulled her up and settled her on his lap. He clamped his hands to her hips, shifting her so that the straining length of his erection pressed against the softness of her centre. Winding her arms around his neck, she lowered her mouth to his and kissed him with such heat that the blood in his veins turned to fire. It spread through his body like a fever, incinerating his bones and draining the strength from his limbs. When they came up for air her breathing was as ragged as his.

'You have no idea how hard it's been resisting you,' he muttered hoarsely as she lifted her hips urgently and he moved one hand between them. 'I thought it would simply be a question of mind over matter. I was wrong. You've been killing me. Another reason I had to leave.'

'I'm glad you're back.'

'So am I.'

She gave a soft moan when he slipped his fingers inside her, trembling in his arms. She writhed against him, panting a little, and their mouths met again, but within seconds there seemed to be an urgency in her that matched the growing desperation in him. Then she moved, he moved and, a moment later, she was sinking onto him, taking him as deep as she could, and everything but her disappeared.

His senses reeled. Her skin was as soft and smooth as satin. Her scent was in his head and her hair felt like silk. Her eyes were dark and wild and locked to his with such heat that surely he was about to combust. She arched her back and breathed 'Unzip me' and he had no issue with that when it meant he could take her nipple in his mouth and tease it until she was begging him for release.

But he was in no mind to grant her wish, so he held her in place and focused on learning the shape and taste of her, every muscle he possessed coiling tighter every time she sighed or gasped or twitched.

Her breathing was shallow and choppy. Her head fell back. He moved his hand down her body, letting it linger for a moment where their baby grew, and then lower, to where they were joined—and with a cry she shattered so powerfully that it triggered his own roaring release. She clung onto him and shook and he hauled her close, pulsating into her hard and deep in a blaze of ecstasy that left him limp and dazed.

When the heat faded and the world swam back into focus, he tipped her off his lap and set her on her feet. Somehow he found the strength to get up himself.

'Follow me,' he muttered, grabbing her hand for support, although whether he was providing it or taking it he wasn't sure.

'Where are we going?'

'I seem to recall you wanting to find out what we could do in a bed.'

CHAPTER TEN

THE FOLLOWING MORNING, Olympia floated down the stairs and into the kitchen as if she was lighter than air.

What a night, she thought, a wide smile spreading across her face as she located a couple of cups, then popped a capsule into the coffee machine and turned it on. She couldn't recall one like it. She'd lost count of the number of times she and Alex had shattered in each other's arms before falling into an exhausted sleep at some time around dawn.

There wasn't an inch of his magnificent body that she hadn't explored. The things he'd done to her—not just in the bed, but also in the shower and on the balcony—would be imprinted for ever on her memory. His muscles were like velvet encased steel. The smattering of coarse dark hair that covered his chest had tickled her skin and electrified her nerve-endings. When he'd set his mouth between her legs and lingered there a while she'd practically jack-knifed off the bed.

Not for one moment did she regret any of it. It had

been so empowering. So deliriously thrilling. And not in the least bit reckless because, unlike on such occasions in the past, she'd given it her full consideration before taking what she wanted.

When he'd told her to go over and get him she could have simply succumbed to the predatory gleam that had appeared in his eye without a second thought. But she hadn't. She'd paused. She'd looked at him across the table, her heart pounding, the excitement whipping through her more stimulating than any drug she'd ever taken, and had asked herself whether she was sure she was doing the right thing. Whether she was really ready to take this step.

Well, she was, she'd decided a moment later, because she'd spent the whole of supper realising that her self-worth *didn't* lie in sex, so she had nothing to fear from it. She wasn't being rash and impulsive. She was making a choice based on a number of well thought through arguments—and what a spectacular choice it had been. Her self-esteem was sky high, and not just because he couldn't get enough of her body. The euphoria she'd experienced had been dazzling but not manic. She really felt as though they were making progress. The concept of being a team was no longer some pipe dream but a very real possibility.

She still had a lot to learn about him of course. Almost everything, in fact, because while she'd

spilled practically the entirety of her soul to him last
night he'd been frustratingly reticent in return. But
now they'd taken the edge off their desire, there'd
be more opportunity for conversation this morning,
she was sure. The emotional connection she wanted
with the father of her child was growing. Trust, even
in its nascent form, truly was a wonderful thing.

A knock at the front door jolted Olympia out of
her dreamy thoughts and she abandoned the coffee for the hall. Two minutes later she'd signed for
two envelopes, one addressed to Alex, the other addressed to her. She placed his on the round marble
table that dominated the space. Hers she took back
to the kitchen to open, and shook out the sheaf of
papers. It looked to be documentation relating to
their marriage and that made her frown. Hadn't he
informed her in no uncertain terms that they were
going to wait?

Maybe he'd reflected on the point she'd made the
morning she'd moved in about implementing their
plans right away and changed his mind. That could
only be a good thing. Whatever the reason behind it,
it proved his commitment to their baby. And to her?
Well, it was early days for them and she mustn't get
ahead of herself, but the signs were there.

So did he have any ideas in mind about what for-
mat the wedding might take, and where? Or would
he give her free rein? She'd have to ask. Not that she
knew what she wanted. She'd never dreamed she'd

146 EXPECTING THE GREEK'S HEIR

ever marry. Although, they'd better do it quickly, because she wasn't sure she wanted to wear a white dress with a massive bump on display.

But hang on. What was this?

Setting aside the contract, Olympia frowned down at the second document in the pack. It appeared to be a prenuptial agreement, which was bizarre when he'd never mentioned one, and money would never be an issue. Even more curiously, there seemed to be only one clause.

Bemused, she scanned it once.

Then again.

And it was on the third reading that everything fell apart.

In the event she messed up in some unspecified way, Alex would divorce her and seek sole custody of their child. She would rescind visitation rights. She would only see her child under a number of very specific circumstances and never on her own. Every decision to be made from there on in would be his.

It was very clear. Very concise. And absolutely brutal.

Olympia's vision blurred and her heart was suddenly beating too fast and too hard. Somehow, she found a stool and managed to sit on it before her legs gave way.

The nightmare scenario she'd told herself couldn't possibly happen the night before had materialised. He *was* planning on taking her child away from her. He didn't trust her at all, she realised, beginning to shake from head to toe as the implications of the prenup sank in and she was filled with roaring emotion. He never had and likely never would. They weren't a team. They weren't anything. He'd even warned her he'd use any weapon at his disposal to get what he wanted, so she didn't know why she was so surprised.

He still thought of her as the wild child she'd once been. She'd never leave her past behind. It would follow her, tainting everything she did, for ever, no matter how much progress she made. And to think that last night she'd actually imagined they'd turned a corner. Just how big a fool was she?

She knew the only person to blame for what had happened here was her. She'd allowed herself to believe that he valued her as an individual rather than just the mother of his child. And a white wedding? *Really?* What had she been *thinking*?

But God it hurt. Her throat was sore and tight. Every cell of her body ached and her heart felt as though it had cleaved in two. She wanted to curl up and cry and then to hit the city. To find the nearest twenty-four-hour club and lose herself in the music. To obliterate the pain with champagne and a line or two. But she couldn't, because she was pregnant and she didn't do that anymore and she would never give him any cause to enact the prenup even if she did sign it.

So she was going to have to deal with this bruising development in a different way. And while it would be the easiest thing in the world to walk out on Alex and his lack of trust, to take her chances and go it alone, her baby needed her to meet the challenges she faced head on. She would *not* let herself revert to her old ways and descend into a seething pit of misery and self-doubt. She could drive herself mad second-guessing what he'd been thinking with this prenup, and those days were over.

Instead, she would bury the anger and pain, channel the determination and tenacity she didn't need him to tell her she had, and find out what he had to say.

Upstairs in the ensuite bathroom, Alex stood beneath the shower, the hot water going some way to ease the pleasant ache in his muscles, and thought that taking Olympia at her word had absolutely been the right thing to do. Twelve hours ago he'd been a man at the end of his tether but now, the mad lust having been dampened, he was back on an even keel. He had no doubt that from here on in the desire would be manageable.

Furthermore, while she'd slumbered beside him, he'd revisited their conversation before supper, finally managing to apply the analysis he was supposedly famed for. He now understood her a whole lot better than he had before. He could see where her insecurities and vulnerabilities stemmed from, and he had renewed admiration for the way she'd pulled herself back from the abyss. Going forward, he would be able to handle whatever she threw at him calmly and objectively. He was back in control of this relationship—and himself—and that was the way things would stay.

Satisfied that he'd one hundred per cent succeeded in the mission he'd embarked upon the night before, and indescribably relieved that she'd sorted out her issues with self-worth, Alex switched off the shower and reached for a towel. He rubbed it over his head, then tied it round his waist and returned to the bedroom—where he found Olympia, sitting on the edge of the bed instead of in it, disappointingly clothed and wearing a blank expression that sent a shiver down his spine.

'What's wrong?' he asked with a frown. When she'd announced she was off to make some coffee she'd had a smile on her face. He was sure of it. He'd put it there only five minutes before.

'While you were in the shower, the paperwork for our marriage was delivered.' Her voice was cold and flat and her body was rigid. 'The contract and your prenup. I gather you've changed your mind about the timeframe. Not that it particularly matters, because I'm signing neither.'

Alex stilled. White noise rushed in his ears and his stomach clenched. He recalled the instructions he'd given to his lawyers back when he'd considered her a loose cannon, and he knew instinctively that this could be bad. Very bad indeed.

'I'd forgotten all about that.'

She stared at him for a moment, pale, stunned, and then her eyes blazed and she shot her feet. 'You forgot that you've decided to weaponise our child?' she asked, blasting him with the full force of her hurt and anger. 'To cut me out of the picture if I make a mistake? How could you be so cruel? What sort of man does that?' She gave her head a sharp furious shake, no longer pale and stunned, but incandescent. 'I can't believe I actually thought we were in this together. I can't believe I thought you trusted me. You even told me you wouldn't hesitate to use my past against me if I dared to defy you. I really am the biggest idiot alive.'

'No,' he said abruptly. 'Stop that. I can explain.'

'How?' She planted her hands on her hips as her chin shot up. 'How can you *possibly* explain what you've done?'

'I ordered the prenup to be drawn up the morning you showed up here and turned my life even more upside down than it already was. At the time it made sense. You'd just told me how vulnerable you were, and the security of our child was my number one priority. You'd said you recognised the danger of relapse. I couldn't risk you taking off on a whim or cutting me out for good.'

'I would never have done that. I told you I needed your support. And I'm well aware of the importance of a stable environment for a child to grow up in.'

'I didn't know that then.'

Her eyebrows arched. 'And you do now?'

'After everything you told me last night, yes.'

'Why should I believe you?'

'Because it's the truth. I meant every word of what I said.'

'No,' she snapped back. 'That's not good enough. You can't expect me to simply take your word for it and just accept your compliments, when for all I know you were just trying to flatter me into bed.'

His jaw clenched. 'I would not do that.'

'So *you* say. But look at it from my perspective. You know practically everything there is to know about me, and all I know about you is that you own and control a billion-euro empire and you're all alone in this world. You've told me nothing about yourself and I've asked time and time again. Your need for control puts your wishes so far above mine they're on another planet. And I realise that I am nothing more to you than the mother of your child, but I won't be able to live like that. I *refuse* to live like that. I deserve respect. So does our child. So if you can't give us that we'd be better off on our own.'

At the thought of Olympia turning on her heel and walking out of his house and his life, something fierce and primitive roared inside him. That wasn't happening. He had to fix this. He had to acknowledge that she had a point. With his reluctance to dive into the trauma of his past he *had* been thinking only of himself. He'd feared an emotional connection developing. Getting in too deep. But he was already up to his neck and that wasn't going to change, so he had to accept he was fighting a losing battle.

She had every right to be angry and hurt. He'd caused her distress, unforgivably if unintentionally triggering her self-esteem issues, and he did not wish to exacerbate it further. He would do whatever it took to prevent her from leaving and taking his future with her, and if that meant talking to her as she had to him, then so be it.

'All right,' he said, folding his arms over his chest and steeling himself for an unpleasant trip down memory lane. 'You wanted to know what the impact of our parents' affair had on me, well, it was, devastating. My upbringing wasn't like yours. It was conventional and uneventful. Until I introduced your mother to my father one school sports day and unleashed carnage. The divorce bankrupted my parents. The stress of it brought on the heart attack that killed my father and reduced my mother to a wreck. I was the one who had to pick up the pieces. I gave up my place at university and took a job that would make me a lot of money fast. Which I did. But it wasn't enough to save the home that had been in my family for generations. And it wasn't enough to stop the cancer that killed my mother two years later.'

'The repercussions lasted years,' he continued, noting that the fire was fading from her gaze, the tension ebbing from her shoulders as he pressed home his advantage. 'I've spent two decades repairing the damage that was done and I won't let history repeat itself by allowing our child to suffer the same fate because of us. So I'll tell you more, Olympia. I'll tell you everything. I'll rip up the prenup and prove to you that you do have my respect. You can have your party and spin it how you wish. You can have whatever you want. But in order for all that to happen, you need to stay.'

What Olympia badly wanted right now was to cling on to the hurt and anger that she'd been wearing like a shield and tell him to get lost. She wanted to protect her damaged self-esteem and convince herself that his opinion of her didn't matter, and that she and her baby really would be fine on their own. She hated and feared the volatility of these feelings that, if she weakened, could have her careening towards a destination she never wanted to revisit.

But she couldn't just selfishly turn round and walk out. She still remained absolutely certain that their baby deserved two functioning parents. And try as she might, she had no argument against his claim that he'd simply arranged the prenup in response to what she herself had told him. She'd have done the same in his position.

In truth, his explanation had taken some of the heat out of her emotions the minute he'd given it. She had to grudgingly admit it had made sense. Now, she'd cooled down enough to realise that by opening the door to his past he'd heard her and afforded her the respect she'd demanded. Whether or not he meant what he said about having whatever she wanted remained to be seen, but he'd seemed to be serious about the party.

So she may have overreacted. She didn't really think he'd flattered her into bed. He'd never given her any reason to doubt the truth of what he said. She had to focus on the last couple of days of this relationship, not the first, and let it go.

They were both taking major steps to make this thing work and she wasn't going to give up the chance to further the emotional connection between them. On the contrary, she was going to do everything in her power to cement it. He'd opened the door to himself and she was going to stride on through.

'Fine.'

CHAPTER ELEVEN

OF COURSE GETTING Alex to open up wasn't that easy. He clearly hadn't talked about his past before. Olympia's questions about his childhood and the fallout of the divorce, as well as the fact that her mother was going to be their child's grandmother, were met with long pauses and deep scowls and he had trouble articulating how he felt about it all. But at least he was trying. And if he resorted to sex whenever she tried to get him to dig deep and expand on his feelings, then that was all right with her, for now. Things were on the right track. They had plenty of time to finesse the conversation.

Now, this Thursday morning, they were travelling by boat to Alex's private island in the Saronic Gulf. He might have agreed to the party, but he'd also told her that he was damned if he was going to have God knew how many Stanhopes invading his home and traipsing across his garden, so it would not be happening there.

As they docked alongside the jetty an hour after departing Piraeus, Olympia looked round and thought that she had no objection whatsoever to his establishing some sort of control over the proceedings. Who would complain about holding a party in such an idyllic spot?

The tiny, isolated landmass was ringed by a beach of golden sand. The water surrounding it shimmered and sparkled in the setting sun, a mesmerising combination of jade, turquoise and azure. Nestled in a forest of trees—at the top of a series of terraces that rose up from the beach—was the house. It was stepped into the lush hillside and had clearly been designed to take full advantage of the views. With its three storeys of clean lines and crisp angles that were held together by acres of sparkling glass, it was a beautiful, very contemporary retreat.

'This is a great venue for the party,' she said, popping on her sunglasses, shading her eyes from the sun's intense reflection, as she disembarked with his help. 'What a house. Modern yet somehow it blends in with the landscape. It's remarkably lovely. Did you build it?'

'I did.' He lifted their luggage out of the boat with barely any effort at all, dumping it on the jetty. 'Or rather, I had it built. Five years ago.'

'Do you entertain here a lot?'

'No.'

'Why not?'

'One, I don't have the time. And two, when I do,

I come here to escape the noise of the city. I come here for the peace.'

Alex alighted and picked up their cases, while Olympia ogled the bunch and flex of his muscles and went weak at the knees.

'I can see the appeal of that,' she said, giving herself a quick shake before they then set off towards land. 'I always adored being surrounded by people. I was hardly ever on my own, but I suspect that was just so I didn't have to think. A distraction from my inner turmoil, if you will.'

'How's your inner turmoil these days?'

'Lessening by the minute. Enough now for me to be able to appreciate peace. How's yours?'

'I don't have any.'

'Are you sure about that?'

'Quite sure. You've therapied it out of me.'

Hmm. She didn't think she had just yet. Still waters ran deep, but she'd get to the bottom of them eventually—for the baby's sake, naturally.

'Well, our guests are going to love this,' she said as the jetty ended and the steps up to the house began. 'Mine will, at least. I'm thinking we can hire a private ferry for the occasion. They could be greeted by fire eaters and raspberry and passion fruit martinis. That should get things going with a bang.'

'I'll have to take your word for it.'

'Do you really not like parties?'

'Not ones filled with Stanhopes.'

'Don't worry, I'll protect you. Someone once told me I'm tough and determined.'

'So I recall.'

'The parties I used to throw were wild,' she said, recalling with a faint wince some of the craziest. 'Once, in Rome, three hundred of us danced the night away in a room with a ceiling painted by Leonardo da Vinci, until one guy started swinging on a chandelier and we got thrown out. I didn't even know half of them. I've been much more ruthless with my guestlist for this party. For a start, I've culled everyone who tried to convince me I didn't need to go rehab. I can't have people like that in my life anymore.'

'No,' he said shortly. 'You can't.'

At his depth of feeling on the subject, she bristled. 'There's no need to be quite so judgemental.'

'I'm not. I simply meant that if anyone so much as dared to try and set you back I'd give them cause to regret it.'

Oh. Right. A curl of warmth unfurled inside her and she inwardly sighed with what felt a lot like envy. 'Our baby is lucky indeed to have such a caring and attentive father.'

For a moment he didn't say anything, just frowned up at the house. 'Are you sure a party is a good idea?'

'It'll be fine,' she reassured him, ignoring the strange ache in her chest and pulling herself together. 'My issues were minor ones and I've been totally sober for months. And don't forget, I'm pregnant. I have an added incentive to steer clear of the booze. But you're sweet to be concerned.'

At that descriptor, his eyebrows shot up. *'Sweet?'* he echoed, clearly appalled.

'Well, perhaps not sweet,' she demurred, thinking of the companies he'd told her he'd taken down and the people who'd crossed him that he'd buried. Back when he'd seethed with hatred and resentment for anyone with her surname, he'd apparently even toyed with the idea of ruining the Stanhope Kallis shipping and banking empire—until he'd realised that its three hundred year history and power that spanned the globe made it frustratingly untouchable. 'I didn't mean to offend. But your concern is misplaced. It's good for my recovery to be in situations that in the past may have caused me grief. I can't avoid social occasions for ever. Nor can you if you're going to be married to me. It'll be fun.'

He emitted a strangled sound that suggested he'd rather chew his own toenails, and she couldn't prevent a small grin. 'So who are you planning to invite?'

'The sort who'll appreciate fire eaters and martinis but wouldn't swing from the chandeliers even if I had any. Assuming they're available with only three days' notice.'

'I've arranged parties with far less than that. Even

if people aren't free, they generally become so. My reputation does have some uses. Any potential gate-crashers I need to be worried about?'

'Such as?'

'Business rivals?'

'No.'

'Spurned girlfriends with a grudge?'

'No girlfriends at all.'

What? Seriously? 'How is that possible?' she asked, unable to keep the incredulity from her voice as they reached the top of the steps, circumnavigating the enormous, very inviting infinity pool. 'I mean, you're handsome and successful, not to mention principled and insightful. You have a protective streak a mile wide, you take your responsibilities seriously and you fight for what's yours. How you have you stayed single all this time?'

'Just lucky I guess.'

At the dry cynicism she could hear in his voice, Olympia frowned. 'Is that really how you view commitment?'

'Up until the afternoon you appeared in my office and forced me to reconsider, yes. I generally work ten hours a day, six, sometimes seven days a week. I'm responsible for eight offices around the world and a thousand staff. My company doesn't run itself. It requires my full attention and always has.'

'It sounds as though I'm not the only one in need of distraction.'

'You couldn't be more wrong,' he countered smoothly. 'There is nothing I need distracting from.'

'Not even loneliness?'

'I don't have time for loneliness. Ask your brother about the pressures of running a global business and the workload. His company is ten times the size of mine.'

'He's also married with a child. He seems to manage.'

'And so will I when the time comes. What was your view of commitment before all this?'

'Oh, I've always been far too much of a handful for anyone to take on for any length of time. I'm only good for one night, two at the most.'

'Don't be ridiculous,' he said as he opened the front door and stood aside to let her in. 'I'm taking you on. Potentially for years.'

'Only because of the baby,' she observed, because it felt necessary to think and say it repeatedly. 'That's who you're really taking on, not me. There's a difference.'

Alex dropped the bags on the pale limestone floor and stared at her for one long moment. His dark eyes glittered as they roamed over her, and quite suddenly Olympia didn't want to talk any more. She didn't want to think about everything that had happened since Friday and why she was here. All she wanted was him.

Her pulse was racing and her mouth was dry,

and it seemed too long since there'd been nothing between them but heat and desire.

'This conversation is over, isn't it?' she asked, her voice thick with the need that she could see reflected in his gaze.

'Yes.'

'Will you show me around?'

'We'll start with the bedroom,' he said, then grabbed her hand and led her up the stairs.

Alex didn't get round to giving Olympia a tour of the rest of the house until later that afternoon, when she told him that her body needed a break and the sex bubble he'd deliberately created to avoid having to think about their conversation on the jetty popped.

How had she managed to stir up so much trouble for him in such a short space of time? he wondered darkly as he left her by the pool and went inside to make the call he could scarcely believe he was about to make. Caring and attentive weren't words he'd ever use to describe himself. And as for friends, commitment, inner turmoil and work as a distraction, well, he didn't tend to dwell on any of that if he could help it. What was the point?

He'd always accepted that he was better off without friends, and the investment of time and energy they'd require with no quantifiable return. Thanks to the breakdown of his parents' marriage he'd spent his entire adult life avoiding commitment like the plague. He'd never been one for navel-gazing. His job required all his attention. And the last thing he wanted to think about was how comprehensively his peace was going to be shattered on Saturday night at eight.

Besides, he'd already come to terms with the ins and outs of throwing this party. He'd have to meet her family at some point, and at least this way he could ensure it happened on his turf, in a place where the air was fresh and he could breathe. He could knock on the head the catchup that Leo had been so keen on, and stamp out the niggle of guilt that he still felt over going behind Olympia's back and calling him up in the first place. In the absence of friends and family he'd invite his clients, both current and prospective, and the useful acquaintances he'd made over the years. He would treat the event as a business opportunity. An occasion to strengthen his connections and therefore his company. Her mother was on the other side of the world, so that was one nightmare he wouldn't have to face just yet, and with any luck, if Olympia was busy organising a party, she wouldn't have time to keep trying to probe into his feelings about the past.

Much to his amazement, sharing with her the details of his life that he'd never shared with anyone before wasn't as traumatic as he'd feared. It was only when she tilted her head and asked him questions such as 'what were some things you liked about that situation?' or 'how do you think you could have handled that differently?' that he froze up. He wasn't used to talking about his emotions, and with her it felt insanely risky to do so.

Luckily, she didn't seem to mind when he distracted her with sex, but he sensed he couldn't put her off for ever. Alarmingly, he increasingly didn't want to. The unfathomable urge to correct her every time she insisted that he was only interested in her because of the baby was growing too.

She wasn't the only loose cannon in this situation, he thought as he brought up the number of Georgiou's, Athens' most exclusive, most discreet jewellers and wondered whether he could actually be losing his mind. She'd upended his life. She tied him in knots. And the truly unsettling thing was that he was beginning to wonder whether part of him actually liked it.

Olympia was on the phone to the event planner the next morning when she heard the rapid *whoop-whoop* sound of an approaching helicopter. Shading her eyes, she looked up to see it pass by overhead—a small metallic dot in a vast expanse of blue—and then turned her attention back to the conversation.

With money no object, arrangements for the party were progressing apace. The DJ, the florist and the pyrotechnician were all booked and on their way. Zander's wife, Mia, a caterer with a flair for the original, was insisting on doing the food despite being on maternity leave, and the world's number one mixologist was being flown in from New York.

Yesterday, when Alex had left her by the pool muttering something about a call, she'd turned her attention to how she might use the party to further her career. When he'd returned, whipping off his T-shirt and stretching beside her on the double sun lounger, she'd wasted no time in outlining his role in her plans.

'I'm looking forward to you meeting Zander,' she'd said, resisting the urge to climb on top of him and assuage the desire that seemed to be getting hotter instead of cooler. 'You can extol my virtues and persuade him to give me the job I really want.'

'What job is that?' he'd said with an oddly inscrutable look in her direction.

'I want to do what you do. I want to manage funds and investments on behalf of other people.'

'Why?'

'I had a lot of time on my hands in the three months I spent in the Arizona desert. I filled it by reading anything I could get hold of, and much of that was material that focused on business. I have no idea why that was the favoured subject matter, but as a result I developed a wholly unexpected interest in finance. I studied market trends and fluctuations. I even identified the sector I found most fascinating—hotels and real estate, weirdly—and devoured as much analysis on it as I could.'

'Identifying the sector one finds the most fascinating and then devouring it seems like a very good idea,' he'd murmured, running his gaze over her bikini-clad body and letting it linger on the parts she knew he liked best.

Olympia had ignored the sizzle of heat that encouraged her to plaster her mouth to his and forced herself to concentrate. 'I have no idea why the idea of making money out of nothing appeals so much, but I came across a programme that allows simulated trading and discovered I have a talent for it. I've been working on gaining the necessary regulatory qualifications and am desperate to put what I've learned into practice. But Zander doesn't think that either I or our clients are quite ready for that. He's insisting I complete a full year drumming up new business before I can move on. A casual word in his ear, telling him how capable I am, repeating all those things you said about me on Tuesday night, wouldn't go amiss. I was also hoping you might share with me everything you know, so that when the time comes I can hit the ground running.'

'You must be mad if you think I'd enable a rival like that.'

'I'm flattered you'd see me as a rival.'

'Stop fishing for compliments. I've already paid you plenty.'

She'd stretched like a cat and given him her most seductive smile. 'I'd make it worth your while.'

'How?'

She'd told him and within seconds he'd leapt off the lounger and dragged her to his study, to share with her some of the finer details of his job. He'd described the speed with which she got to grips with spreads and returns on investments as remarkable. Her ability to correctly apply external events to market movements was apparently uncanny. They hadn't got round to discussing client management, because by that point she'd been overcome with the need to express her appreciation, and he'd had her flat on her back on his desk a moment later.

Fifteen minutes after she finished her conversation with the event planner, Alex materialised on the terrace where she sat, looming over her like a pillar at the Temple of Apollo, and said, 'You have a visitor.'

'The helicopter?'

He nodded and Olympia frowned, sitting up a little straighter in her chair. In approximately thirty-six hours the island would be a hive of activity, but everyone involved in the setting up of the party would be arriving by boat, and she wasn't expecting anyone else.

'Who?' she asked, squinting up at him and hoping to God it wasn't her mother, who was supposed to be on the other side of the world, but with Selene, one never quite knew.

'It occurred to me that if you want to put on a show on Saturday night, you'll need an engagement ring. So I've had a selection flown over from Athens from which you can take your pick.'

Before she could react, he turned abruptly and gave a short nod. A man in an immaculately tailored pale grey suit, holding a silver briefcase, stepped into her line of sight. Behind him moved two other taller and bulkier men, both wearing black suits, sunglasses and earpieces. 'This is Aristotle Georgiou.'

Olympia recognised the name if not the face, and as he and Alex sat down beside her, her heart began to beat unnaturally fast. A ring? From one of the world's most prestigious jewellers? For her?

'How very thoughtful,' she murmured, trying to contain the dangerous thrills that were suddenly shooting through her.

'Hmm.'

Aristotle Georgiou set the case on the table and unlocked it. When he opened the lid she couldn't help but gasp. In front of her was the most dazzling array of diamonds, sapphires, rubies and emeralds she'd ever seen. She was no stranger to wealth and extravagance. Her mother's jewellery collection was allegedly worth billions. But these pieces were something else. Stones the size of coins flashed in the sun with a brilliance that was blinding. The gold and platinum in which they were set had been polished to a shine that gleamed. Each one was an exquisite work of art that for some bizarre reason brought tears to her eyes.

And she would have assumed that it would be easy to choose one because it wasn't as if the ring meant anything. It was simply for show and she knew that. So in theory all she had to do was close her eyes, pick one out at random and then put it on her finger.

But she couldn't. She couldn't move. She could barely even breathe. The only thought now banging around her head was, what if this were for real? What if Alex loved her and she loved him and this— the first piece of jewellery she'd ever been given— mattered?

For one electrifying moment the world tilted on its axis. The terrace beneath her feet disappeared. She'd never wanted anything so badly. To be loved and valued and the centre of someone's world—the idea of it made her head spin like a top and her heart ache so hard that she was in pain.

But she had to get a grip, she told herself frantically, fighting for control before she mortified herself by blubbing. That wasn't for her. She must never make the mistake of thinking any of what was happening here was for real. This relationship had been born out of necessity and that was all. Alex didn't want *her*. He didn't love her and she wasn't the centre of his world. By providing her with a ring, he was merely doing her a favour. It *didn't* matter, and she must not forget that.

'This one will do,' he said, his voice slicing through the thundering haze in her head as he plucked a ring from the case, evidently fed up with her inability to decide. 'It suits your colouring and passionate personality.'

'An emerald-cut red diamond solitaire set in a band of twenty-four-carat gold,' intoned the jeweller as Alex unceremoniously took her left hand and stuck it on her finger. 'Simple yet stunning. Very rare. An excellent choice.'

It was, Olympia thought, swallowing hard as she stared down at the ring, turned her hand this way and that, and tried not to like it too much. It fitted her finger perfectly. It sparkled like fire. She couldn't have chosen better herself.

But she must not overthink his reasons for choosing it, which, although hardly romantic, weren't random at all. She must not let herself be overtaken by what-ifs. Because if she did, if she wasn't careful and started to read more into this than there was, she could find herself in a whole heap of trouble.

CHAPTER TWELVE

AT TEN ON Saturday evening, Olympia stood at the top of the steps, in the flickering shadows, and gazed out over the terraces that cascaded down to the beach. She might be a screwup, she thought as she surveyed the scene with a warm ripple of pleasure, but she did know how to throw a party.

The event planner, who'd been working his socks off since first thing this morning, was worth every cent of his extortionate fee. Torches lined the jetty and the steps up to the house. Strings of lights edged the beach and draped through the trees. The pool shimmered like liquid jade, and around it sat tubs of myrtle perfuming the air. A DJ was playing music that had a sultry samba beat, which had the guests swaying, and the delicious food that her sister-in-law had provided was going down a treat.

For all Alex's misgivings, she wasn't tempted by any of the free-flowing alcohol. Once upon a time she'd got through a bottle of champagne a night with no problem at all, but she hadn't touched a drop of anything stronger than tonic water in a year, pregnant or not. She was perfectly happy with a margarita mocktail, especially since he'd rejected raspberry and passion fruit in favour of an alcohol-free beer, in what he'd described as a sign of solidarity. And that wasn't the only difference about this party. She was genuinely enjoying herself. She wasn't pretending to have a good time to mask the fact that she was miserable. In fact, the whole vibe of the evening was giving her a lovely warm glow.

Or perhaps that was the ring that she'd hardly been able to take her eyes off since he'd put it on her finger. Every time she looked at it she caught some new spark of fire, some new hue to its colour. With the sun on it, the stone shone light and clear. Now, as night fell and the stars came out, its rich dark tones made her think of intoxicating sensuality and heady desire. Of the twisted sheets and ragged breathing and wild abandonment she'd experienced with him last night, which had somehow felt more intense than before.

Beneath the moonlight, in between catching their breath and the rise of relentless desire, he'd told her about his need for financial security as a result of his parents' ruinous divorce. About how he'd been given a position in a bank by a sympathetic family friend and had turned out to have a knack for investment. The foreign markets in particular had become his playground, and within a year he'd made a cool five million. A decade later, he'd established his own funds, which traded a wide range of products on behalf of some of the richest people in the world.

He'd elaborated on his friendship with her brother, and the affair. Finally able to talk a little about his feelings, he'd confessed to the guilt he felt about introducing her mother to his father and the anger and resentment that had combined with the grief of losing both his parents. Olympia had tried to convince him that it wasn't his fault, but she didn't know if she'd succeeded. Nor did she have any further insight into how he felt now about her mother. He must have hated her at the time, and he obviously still harboured some ill will towards her, but to what extent? She'd asked but he'd prevaricated and she wondered if, perhaps, he didn't know either.

Now, instinctively, she sought him out, and her gaze landed on him almost immediately, because all evening she'd been aware of where he was. He was wearing a dark suit and an open-necked white shirt, and he looked so stunningly handsome that her breath caught in her throat for so long she went a little dizzy.

A moment ago, he'd been chatting to her brother, Leo, and before that, Zander. But now he was on his own once again, standing at the edge of the section of the beach that had been converted into a dancefloor, hands in his pockets, staring out to sea, and it struck her suddenly how very much alone he really was.

Most of the guests here were hers—friends, colleagues, all five of her siblings with their respective spouses. The few he'd invited seemed to be related to his business in some way. Even the Sheikh had put in a brief appearance, before being whisked away by his security detail. But when she'd subtly probed—while they'd all lauded his business acumen and success—none of them had been able to shed any light on him personally.

She knew he had no family, and that was hardly his fault, but why did he have no friends? Why would anyone want to live like that? What was the real reason behind his avoidance of commitment? Surely it couldn't just be the demands of his job. And how did he actually feel about marrying her and fathering a child if he genuinely preferred his own company?

'Great party.'

These words, delivered in a familiar drawl, jolted Olympia out of her tumbling thoughts and she determinedly shook them off because tonight wasn't a night for such weighty ruminations. Tonight was a celebration. Or rather, she speedily amended as she turned to see that Zander had joined her at the balustrade, a *performance*.

'It is, isn't it?' she asked, the pride and pleasure with which she'd been regarding the proceedings faltering a fraction, before she forced herself to rally.

'Of course, I'd expect nothing less,' Zander said

dryly. 'I thought I was a party animal, but you took it to a whole other level.'

'Not any more. You can't deny this is eminently civilised.'

'I wouldn't dream of it. It's the height of sophistication.' He looked at her shrewdly. 'So how are you coping?'

'Absolutely fine,' she said, slightly surprised by the question, which indicated a level of interest she'd learned not to expect. But then she hadn't envisaged all siblings plus in-laws turning up here tonight either, so who knew what was going on. 'Most of what I used to get up to was for show anyway. Rehab was more of a reset than a cure.'

'It did you good.'

'I know.'

Zander's expression turned unusually thoughtful as he folded his arms across his chest and leaned back against the balustrade. 'I was cornered by your new fiancé earlier.'

'I saw.'

'His reputation for ruthlessness precedes him, and I wouldn't want to get on the wrong side of him businesswise, but he seems like a decent enough guy. He can't sing your praises highly enough.'

At that, her eyebrows shot up and her heart skipped a quick beat. 'Oh?'

'I've been hearing all about your skill and tenacity, and the work you've been putting in to passing your exams. I understand he's shared with you all the trading tips he's picked up over the years. He's your biggest fan. He said that I was an idiot for not deploying your many talents in a more productive role, and that if I didn't give you the asset management job you want, he would.'

For a moment Olympia couldn't believe what she was hearing. Yes, she'd asked Alex to put in a good word for her, but she hadn't actually thought he'd do it. Was he simply holding up his side of the bargain, or did he genuinely believe her capable of doing the job she so badly wanted? Had he *fought* for her?

'Can you imagine the optics of that?' she said lightly while her mind raced, trying but failing to work out what it meant. 'The press would have a field day. It was bad enough when you hired me.'

'You may have a point,' Zander agreed with a nod. 'But he does too. You've done really well these past few months. I'm impressed. I should have seen it sooner, and I probably would have without the severe sleep deprivation a newborn baby brings. You'll find that out soon enough. Call me on Monday and we'll talk about your next move.'

'That would be great,' she said, noting not only the shadows beneath her brother's eyes but also the quiet way he seemed to light up at the mention of his tiny son, and wondering how Alex would feel when the time came. 'Thank you, Zander. I won't let you down.'

'You're welcome. I know you won't. But, although I'd like to take the credit, it's not me you should be thanking.'

Two hours into the party, Alex had to admit that it wasn't nearly as grim as he'd initially feared, but that was probably because he wasn't giving it his full attention. Even the endless stream of congratulations, which he'd assumed would have brought him out in hives, had failed to make much of an impression. He was too busy contemplating the ring.

If he'd ever thought that the outcome of selecting a purely functional engagement ring merited any consideration, prior to Aristotle Georgiou's trip to his island, he would have assumed that once he'd dispatched the jeweller back to Athens that would have been that. He'd decided Olympia needed a prop and he'd got her one. Job done. He would not have anticipated it still playing on his mind some thirty-six hours later, yet it did.

Why, when she'd dithered and he'd had to step in before they both ossified where they sat—or worse, she made the wrong choice—had his involvement in the selection felt somehow portentous? Why, when instinct had told him, *this one,* had he for one mad moment wondered whether that instinct referred to the ring or the woman who'd be wearing it? And why did he feel such deep satisfaction whenever he caught her looking at it?

Initially, he'd simply pushed these frustratingly baffling questions from his head and forced himself to think instead about how brewing political unrest in various corners of the globe might affect his vast portfolio of funds. When the event organisers had shown up, and he'd immediately felt the beginnings of a headache, he'd escaped to the gym to sweat out his tension on the treadmill.

But later he'd taken her to bed, and for some reason the bloody ring had flashed like a beacon all sodding night, loosening his inhibitions and his tongue, and he might as well not have bothered with any of it. Had he had to share with her his innermost feelings about pretty much everything under the sun? No, he had not. But, as if she'd spiked him with some sort of truth drug, he'd barely been able to stop talking at all.

The insane disruption of the last day and a half had transformed his estate into some sort of dark twinkly flickering wonderland. With lights festooned about the place and artfully positioned pieces of furniture and random greenery, the gardens had never looked so appealing.

Nor had Olympia.

In a red knee-length halter-neck dress that she'd had sent over first thing this morning—because it apparently went with the ring that was causing him so much grief—she looked so stunning she took his breath away. Every time he caught sight of her he thought that his architecturally significant house wasn't the only remarkably lovely thing on the island.

As life and soul of the party, she was also in her element, chatting and laughing and making sure that everyone was having a good time, while attracting attention like moths to a flame. How she knew so many people he had no idea. She obviously collected them, and the thought that this might be his life from now on made him feel faint.

But at least the dreaded bombardment of memories hadn't materialised. All five of her siblings were here, which was a surprise when she'd implied that three of them would be unable to attend, but talking to them had been so uneventful he'd found himself wondering what on earth he'd been thinking all these years. There was nothing monstrous about any of them. They were all as perfectly normal as the next ultra-rich person. Zander had taken on board his observations about Olympia's many talents and how they might be of benefit to him with no problem at all.

In fact, the only conversation that had proved bothersome so far was the one he'd had with the Sheikh. 'Many congratulations on your forthcoming nuptials to Miss Stanhope,' Abdul Karim had said with a smile that had then turned disconcertingly knowing. 'I sensed something was up in Switzerland. Such sparks. I knew instantly that no one would be having dinner with her but you. I am never wrong about these things.'

Alex didn't know what exactly the Sheikh thought he could see. Although their chemistry was still pretty volatile, despite their very best efforts to dampen it, so perhaps that was the giveaway. But thankfully he hadn't been able to give the matter any further thought because Leo had then appeared at his side for the catchup he'd mentioned on the phone.

'Good to see you,' had been his former best friend's opening salvo as he'd clapped him on the back and shaken his hand. 'It's been a while.'

'Twenty years.'

'How have you been?'

'Good. You?'

'Great. Happy on Santorini building boats. Married. Two daughters. Hard to believe when you think about the things we used to get up to.'

'I'm sorry I cut you off so abruptly back then,' Alex had said with a frown, as Olympia's censure of how he'd handled the situation came back to him. 'But Selene destroyed my family. It left us all broken. I did what I had to do.'

Leo had looked at him shrewdly. 'I get that. Although it took me some time to work it out. I was sorry to hear about your parents.'

'I was sorry to hear about your father.'

'I could have done with a friend then,' Leo had

said with a shrug. 'As could you, no doubt. But I've never seen much point in regret.'

'Nor me.'

'So you and Olympia… It's not just a convenience thing, is it?'

'What makes you say that?'

'You can't keep your eyes off each other.'

First the Sheikh, now Leo. What could they see that he couldn't?

'It's complicated,' Alex had muttered by way of prevarication.

'It always is.'

They'd chatted for a while longer, catching up on the last twenty years, and then Leo had sauntered off to find his wife, leaving Alex to ruminate on what his friend had said about the nature of his relationship with Olympia. It had changed over the last couple of days, he thought as he rubbed a hand along his jaw. He'd started talking about his feelings and the world hadn't imploded, even though he'd found it impossible to accept her perspective. So perhaps it was developing into one that went beyond mere convenience.

How he felt about that, however, he'd have to park for later analysis, because Olympia was making a beeline for him with a determined yet dreamy look on her face, which he couldn't understand, but nevertheless it tightened his chest and constricted his lungs. The wave of emotion that he couldn't even begin to identify swept through him like a river bursting its banks, and nearly took out his knees.

But then something over his shoulder caught her eye and she stopped dead in her tracks, the dreaminess turning first to shock and then to appal. He glanced round to see what was causing her such consternation, fully prepared to come to her rescue if required, and then it was his turn to freeze.

Because coming to a whiplash of a stop at the end of the jetty, sending waves tumbling to the shore, was a speedboat. And being helped off that speedboat a moment later was a woman, swathed in gold lamé and draped in diamonds, a woman who looked not a day over forty even though she had to be in her mid-sixties.

Her mother.

His nemesis.

The very much uninvited, deeply unwelcome Selene Stanhope.

CHAPTER THIRTEEN

OH, DEAR GOD, thought Olympia, watching in abject horror as her mother sashayed along the jetty as if she were on the red carpet at some international film premiere. What the hell was she doing here? Why wasn't she in Argentina with her cattle billionaire? And how on earth had she found out about the party?

More pressingly how was she—Olympia—going to handle it? Unsurprisingly, in a crowd of two hundred, Leo and Zander—who were more used to dealing with this than she was—were nowhere to be seen. But a quick glance at Alex, standing there on the beach, frozen to the spot, his jaw so tight it looked as though it might be about to shatter, told her that despite his claims to the contrary, he evidently wasn't as blasé about the affair as he'd tried to make out. And, therefore, she knew without the shadow of a doubt that her mother could not stay.

Having no time to ponder the fact that her loyalty fell so unquestionably in his camp, or to wonder what that might mean, she galvanised into action,

hurried down the steps and onto the jetty, to inter-
cept Selene before she could do too much damage.

'Darling,' cried her mother expansively, as she
threw open her arms for a hug that she had never
earned and was never going to get. 'I heard you were
having a party to celebrate your engagement. The
last of my children to fly the nest. My littlest one.
I've come to offer you my congratulations. A whirlwind engagement and a baby on the way. Quick
work. That's my girl. I'm so proud. And to think I
was worried you'd become boring.'

This outpouring of maternal interest—all for
show, of course—did not faze Olympia in the slight-
est. Nor did the dig about the changes she'd made to
her life, or the suggestion that they were alike. The
only thing she was interested in was containing the
chaos that Selene whipped up wherever she went,
and then finding out if Alex was all right.

'You need to leave,' she said, taking her mother
by the arm and wheeling her back in the direction
she'd come.

'But I've only just arrived.'

'You weren't invited.'

'I assumed it was an oversight.'

'It wasn't.'

'Well, this wasn't the welcome I was expecting, I must say,' protested her mother with a pout.
She broke free and tried to bypass Olympia to join

the party. 'But no matter. I'm here now to liven things up.'

'Get back on the boat and off my island, Selene.'

The sudden appreciative gleam in her mother's eyes, as much as the cold clipped tones, told Olympia that Alex was behind her. A fierce streak of protectiveness swept through her and she instinctively inched closer to him.

'Are you the groom?' asked Selene, running her gaze over him with such outrageously blatant interest that Olympia wanted to push her into the sea. 'Well done, Olympia. He's very handsome. In fact,' she said, tilting her head suddenly and giving him as thoughtful a look as her overly Botoxed face would allow, 'he looks like someone I used to know a long time ago. Let me think…'

'I really wouldn't,' Olympia warned, glancing at Alex, noting both the ice-cold fury burning in his eyes and the seething tension he radiated.

'Nikolas Andino, I believe it was,' said Selene, blithely blind to the danger she was in. 'Any relation?'

'I'm his son.'

'Ah, yes. Now I remember. Weren't you once a friend of Leo's?'

'Until you blew my family apart.'

'Did I? Well, these things happen,' she said with a dismissiveness that was shocking, even for her. 'But goodness,' she added, a hideously inappropriate twinkle now lighting her eyes, 'if I were twenty years younger and you weren't marrying my daughter and I didn't have scruples… Now, who's going to get me a drink?'

'No one,' he said. 'You are not staying.'

'That's what I said,' Olympia put in, feeling sick to her stomach at her mother's callousness and her flirting. *Scruples? If only.* 'I'm having trouble making her listen.'

'No problem.'

Without preamble, he stepped forward and picked Selene up in his arms and then dumped her back in the boat. 'Take her back,' he said to the driver, in a tone that had the man nodding frantically and hastily loosening the lines. 'Do not return.'

'Well. I don't think I've ever been treated so rudely,' Selene exclaimed as he pulled in the fenders and fired the engine. 'Do not expect my presence at the wedding.'

'We won't.'

Heart pounding and head spinning, Olympia watched the boat disappear into the distance, then turned to the big angry man beside her, whose opinion of her mother was now blindingly obvious.

'So that was clearly as horrendous for you as it was for me,' she said, awash with concern for him— for them—and the need to do whatever it took to make this right. 'Are you OK?'

'I'm fine,' he said, and off he stalked.

* * *

But Alex wasn't fine. He wasn't fine at all. He felt as if he was about to throw up. Pass out. As if he were having an out of body experience. Somehow he managed to hold it together as he weaved his way through the guests, smiling here, muttering a suitable response there. But the minute he reached his study, all semblance of composure disappeared.

With shaking hands, he cracked open a bottle of whisky he'd swiped from the kitchen en route through the house. He filled a glass and knocked it back, but the alcohol that burned down his throat and hit his stomach did nothing to numb the shock of seeing the woman who'd destroyed his parents' marriage and wrecked his life.

The second he'd laid eyes on her he'd been slammed back to the past, to the arguments and the tears, the giving up of his place at university, the devastating realisation that his father was human, just as susceptible to all the frailties that implied as anyone else. He was filled with the fiery cocktail of emotions that he'd told Olympia about but hadn't experienced in years—guilt, anger, resentment, fear. If he'd had any doubt whatsoever about how he still felt about Selene Stanhope, it had gone. He seethed with rage. He loathed her with a passion. Twenty years seemed to have vanished, just like that.

The door opened. He first stiffened, then jerked his head round to see Olympia walk in.

'I'm so sorry about that,' she said before he could tell her to get out and leave him alone. 'I had no idea she was going to turn up. I genuinely thought she was safely several thousand miles away.'

He poured himself another measure and downed that in one too. 'I don't want to talk about it.'

'I know you don't,' she said, the concern he detected in her voice as unwanted and unwelcome as the pity he could see on her face. 'But I think you should.'

'No.'

'Please. Tell me how you feel. You need to deal with this.'

He did not need to deal with this, he had too many feelings to manage, and he did not need her telling him what to do. 'Stop it,' he said, his pulse hammering at his temple so loudly he could hear it. 'Stop trying to get inside my head.'

'I want to help.'

But he didn't want her help. Not now. Not ever. He never had, yet somehow she'd demolished every one of his carefully erected barriers so that he was doing everything she asked of him. Suddenly it was all too much. He was being thwacked over the head with the terrible realisation that history was repeating itself. Everything he'd feared had come to pass. Look at how swiftly he'd fallen under her spell. How easily he'd been seduced. She'd wrapped him around her finger with no trouble at all, even though he'd sworn that that would never happen, and he'd been so overwhelmed by lust, by her, he'd just let it all happen. He'd even told her she could have whatever she wanted. What the hell had he been doing this past week?

'I'm done dancing to your tune,' he said, suddenly feeling very cold and numb.

She paled. 'What do you mean?'

'Your mother implied that you were like her, and she was right. You have the same allure, the same power. Just as she trapped my father in her web, you've caught me in yours. You've had me doing things I never had any intention of doing. You've turned me into someone I don't recognise, and I won't allow it to continue.'

For a moment, she appeared to have nothing to say. Her eyes swam with hurt and confusion, and he steeled himself not to care.

'Is that really what you think?'

'Yes.'

'Well, that's not very fair.'

His brows snapped together. 'What?'

'You don't strike me as a man who does anything he doesn't want to,' she said with a jut of her chin, the hurt and confusion morphing into resolve right in front of him. 'You're not passive in any way. You don't *let* things happen to you. If you go along with something it's because you want to. I admit to provoking you into action on occasion, but you didn't have to suggest marriage. You didn't have to buy me a ring. And you certainly didn't have to put in a good word with Zander, although I am grateful for that. I may resemble my mother, and I may have once behaved a bit like she does, but I'm not like her. I refuse to be. Not just for my own sense of self, but because I want my child to have a better start in life than I did. I want it to know love and security, to have a better mother than I do, and to never have to question its self-worth. We've moved way beyond this, Alex. So don't think I don't know what you're doing here.'

'What's that?'

'You're deflecting.'

He scowled at her. 'What makes you the expert?'

'I learned all about it in rehab. It's a defence mechanism. You're in shock, being battered by painful memories, and you're taking it out on me. And that's fine. For now. I understand. But you need to get over the issues you have with my mother. And you *must*,' she entreated. 'For the baby's sake. For my sake and yours and ours. I know she's a nightmare, and she's caused you untold misery, but we have a real shot at this. Neither of us needs to be lonely any more. We have a connection that goes beyond the baby, and we can build on that. So put your past behind you as I did mine. Look forwards, not backwards. It's been twenty years. Move on. Let it go.'

For a moment, Alex could do no more than reel.
His breath was stuck in his throat. He felt as though
he'd been hit with a hammer. *Let it go? Was she serious?*

'I can't *let it go*,' he said, so scathingly that she
flinched. 'It's part of who I am and always will be.
My entire adult life has been based on it. I never
asked for an emotional connection and I certainly
don't want one. I won't be enslaved by you, Olympia. I won't be spat out when you're done, as your
mother did to my father. I hate the way you make
me feel. The lust I have for you threatens my control
and destroys my reason. That's why I snubbed you
the night we met. Why I left you in the stairwell in
Switzerland. You make me do things I'm not proud
of. Believing I could control it was a mistake. *We*
are a mistake.'

She was as white as a sheet. 'You can't mean
that.'

'I do.' He'd never meant anything more in his
life. 'But it's not unfixable. You can move out of my
house and back to yours. In due course, we will call
off the engagement. There's still plenty of time to
come to some arrangement over the baby. There's
no reason we can't be civilised about this. In the
meantime, however, I'd like to be left alone.'

Stunned and shaken, Olympia left Alex's study and
stumbled to the cloakroom, where she was violently

sick. Somehow she made it up the stairs, into the bedroom they were sharing and sank down onto the bed. Outside, the party was in full swing, but how could return to it when her world had just fallen apart? How could she chat and smile and radiate happiness when inside she was in pieces?

He resented her allure.

He hated the way she made him feel.

He didn't want any sort of relationship with her.

How was she to stand it when, for her, with regards to all these points, the opposite was true?

She'd thought the prenup had caused her excruciating pain, but that was nothing compared with the indescribable agony she was feeling now. It was as if he'd reached into her chest and ripped out her heart. She'd never cried, not once, not even as a kid, yet now tears were leaking out of her eyes like the Haliacmon.

And it wasn't because her reputation would suffer from a broken engagement. Or because she feared for the future of their child.

It was because she'd fallen in love with him.

Over the last week, he'd come to mean everything to her. He'd given her all the things she'd been missing her entire life. He'd built up her self-esteem and uncovered her worth. He'd fought in her corner and shown her respect. The protectiveness he'd displayed towards their child had assured her that her upbringing hadn't been normal, and her response to it had not been her fault. He'd made her feel valued, special, cared for.

And to have it suddenly snatched away was like losing a limb.

He'd told her she could have whatever she wanted, but that wasn't true. She wanted him and he wasn't hers. But then why would he be? She was a bad return on investment and always had been. What had made her think she deserved to love and be loved anyway? To dream that, like Zander and Mia, she and Alex might find happiness after being brought together by an unexpected pregnancy? How could she have been so deluded?

But those were questions for later, she thought with a sniff and a blow of her nose. She could regret her loyalty, her defence of him and her stupidity another time. Right now, she had to figure out what to do. She couldn't stay here with a man who didn't want her. So she'd go back to the party and see it through. It wouldn't be the first time she'd put on a show while dying inside. And at the end of the night, mercifully soon, she'd pack up her things and stow away on one of the ferries returning the guests to the mainland. Once home she would lick her wounds in private and figure out how to proceed from there.

Giving herself a shake and taking a deep steadying breath, Olympia got to her feet. She powdered her nose, fluffed out her hair and practised her smile until it looked natural not manic. And then, summoning up every drop of strength and composure she possessed, calling on resources she hadn't had cause to use in a year, she headed downstairs.

CHAPTER FOURTEEN

ON AN INTELLECTUAL LEVEL, Alex knew that beyond the walls of his study the party was still going on, even if he couldn't hear it over the chaos screaming through his head. But it hardly registered. All he could focus on was the conversation that had just taken place and still thundered through his thoughts.

He'd been absolutely right to cool things down with Olympia, he assured himself grimly as, through the window, he watched a firework shoot into the sky and explode into a shower of glittering stars. They'd been moving too far and too fast. If he'd allowed the relationship to continue as it was, he had no doubt he would have been signing himself up for untold misery.

So why did he feel as though he'd been gutted like a fish? Why did he feel he'd be haunted for the rest of his days by the devastation on her face?

He couldn't seem to shake the points she'd made from his head. All he could think now was that the man he didn't recognise wasn't the one she'd turned him into, but the one he'd described as himself. That man sounded weak and powerless, and that *wasn't* him. So perhaps he *had* been lashing out at her, which *wasn't* fair.

And those observations weren't the only ones spinning through his thoughts on some torturous, relentless loop. No matter how hard he tried to shut it up, an irritating voice in his head demanded to know whether, despite the discouraging risk–reward ratio of friends, he was really content existing in isolation.

Might he in fact use work to stave off loneliness? Why had he wanted to refute her repeated declarations that he was only interested in their baby? Where had the shudder he'd always experienced at the thought of being connected to her for years gone? And if he was really so averse to romantic commitment, then why had Olympia's 'we's and 'our's given him such a kick these past few days?

Because he was in love with her.

The thought shot through his head like an arrow, and lodged in his brain. Every muscle in his body froze.

No. He couldn't be. It was impossible. He'd spent his entire life avoiding such a fate. He'd seen the damage love could do when it failed. He knew how fickle and treacherous the heart was. He'd sworn never to hand responsibility for his well-being and happiness to someone else for them to destroy.

But that insidious little voice was once again hammering him with questions and demanding answers. What if love didn't tear you apart but built you up? What if a heart could be steadfast and true? And what if that someone else didn't wreck your well-being and happiness, but treasured and nurtured it?

How Olympia had felt about him before he'd ruined what had been developing he had no idea. Could she be in love with him too? Had the moment with the engagement ring been as significant for her as it had for him? She'd stood up for him. She'd convinced him that he could be the sort of father he was determined to be. He'd done the same for her, and he wasn't finished. He wanted to prove to her that she was worth more than one or two nights— that she might be a handful but she was his handful. He wanted her in his life for ever, stirring up his boring staid existence like a tornado. He wanted this child of theirs to be the first of many, to create a big noisy family of his own.

But, by needing to keep himself safe—by being completely blind to not only what the Sheikh and Leo had seen, but also in his violent reaction to the engagement ring—he'd destroyed any chance of it. He'd put his fears, his needs, above all else, which meant that he was no better than his father. History *was* repeating itself and he was at the root of it, so he was the only person who could do anything about it.

Olympia was right, he thought, his head spinning, his chest tight. He did have to get over the issues he had with his father and Selene. He did have to let it go and focus on the family he could have, rather than the one he'd lost. As she had, with the past and the prenup. She didn't dwell or stew. She moved on. She had more courage in her little finger than he did in his entire body. She was magnificent.

And he'd told her they were a mistake.

He'd told her she was just like her mother.

He was in love with her and he'd told her that he hated it.

What the hell had he done?

An image of her face, pale and wrecked, flashed before his eyes, and Alex felt an ice-cold sweat break out all over his skin. Nausea rolled up his throat. Whatever she felt for him, she cared enough to be hurt. He had to fix the mess he'd made. She was too important to lose. And to think that he'd assumed she'd be the one to screw up. How much more of a jackass could he be?

He surged to his feet and went in search of her. She wasn't in the house. Or on the terraces. He found her down on the beach, surrounded by a group of guests, and never had he wanted to get rid of a bunch of people more. To the untrained eye, the smile on her face would be blinding. But to him it looked like a struggle. There was a sheen to her eyes that suggested she'd been crying, and the realisation that he'd done that to her cut him to the bone.

'Olympia.'

'Ah, here he is,' she said smoothly, as if the conversation in his study had never happened. 'Everyone was wondering where you'd got to.'

'Just taking a moment to sort a few things out,' he said, regret and the need to put this right battering him hard. 'If you'll excuse us, I'd like a word with my fiancée.'

'We mustn't neglect our guests.'

'They can spare us for a few moments.'

'Maybe later.'

'This can't wait.'

Before she could protest further, he took her elbow and steered her away.

'Once again, you're wheeling me away from a party,' she said with a tonelessness that he didn't like one little bit, but for which he had only himself to blame. 'And look what happened the last time you did that.'

'Best move of my life.'

'What?'

Behind the tree he'd led her to, he let her go and rubbed his hands over his face, before thrusting them in the pockets of his trousers.

'I apologise for earlier,' he said gruffly. 'I didn't mean any of it. You were right. I was thrown by your mother showing up. I handled it badly. So very badly.'

She shrugged and stared at a point somewhere over his left shoulder. 'It's fine.'

'It's not fine. It's not fine at all.'

'It really doesn't matter.'

'It does. There's more. So much more I have to apologise for and tell you.'

'But I don't want to hear it,' she said, her gaze finally meeting his, shaking him to the core with its emptiness. 'In fact, I don't want to hear anything you have to say. I'm not interested in your apologies or anything else. I'm done, Alex. You wanted me gone and I'm going. The minute this party's over, I'm leaving. This is the last time we'll speak until the baby's born. We can communicate through our lawyers when necessary.' She glanced over her shoulder. 'Now I really must get back to the party.'

She disappeared before he had time to blink, let alone think. He could barely breathe through the panic that gripped him at the thought that he'd blown it for good, let alone muster up a response. But as the fog in his head cleared, he was filled with the resolve that had made him a billionaire before he hit thirty.

If she thought this was the last time they spoke, she could think again. They would not be communicating through lawyers. She was leaving over his dead body. And she would absolutely hear what he had to say.

Back in the thick of things, Olympia took a surreptitious look at her watch. Half an hour to go. Half an hour until this ridiculously painful charade was over and she could go home.

If she'd known how difficult it was going to be to endure the congratulations and the increasing raucousness of the occasion she'd have remained holed up in the bedroom, because there was absolutely nothing to celebrate. But at least she'd stayed strong when Alex had dragged her off for a word. At least she hadn't broken down and begged him for a second chance. She'd never have got over the humiliation.

It was bad enough that she hurt so much, she thought, her throat aching from all the lumps she'd had to swallow down. She was so stupid for letting him get to her. For caring what he thought about her. She should have got used to rejection by now. She should have remembered that affection was never freely given. For years she'd avoided transferring her neediness onto a man for fear of the inevitable rejection, but she'd done it anyway. She was her own worst enemy in practically every way there was.

The music ground to a halt. Everyone hushed. She turned to see Alex behind the DJ's decks, holding the microphone and staring straight at her and, *oh, God,* what was going on now? Was he about to reveal that the engagement was off? Was her reputation once again about to be decimated? Where could she run? Where could she hide?

'I'd like to propose a toast,' he said, and she

thought despairingly, to what? A lucky escape and freedom? The ruthless destruction of someone he hated? 'To my bride-to-be, Olympia Stanhope, with whom I'm head over heels in love.'

Her heart stopped. Her breath caught in her throat. All the blood rushed to her feet and she very nearly swooned. But these were just fine words, she reminded herself, and he wasn't to be trusted, not after the cruel things he'd hurled at her in his study. He wasn't in love with her. He couldn't be. It made no sense.

'She won't believe that,' he said, as if he could read her mind. 'I haven't made it easy. In fact, I may well have made it impossible. I've said some terrible things, and the apologies I owe her are too many to count. But I will address every single one of them, however long it takes, if she'll give me the chance.' He visibly swallowed and, when he continued, it was with a crack in his voice. 'Olympia, you are the strongest, bravest woman I've ever met. You are clever and resourceful and you don't give up. You have repeatedly blown me away with your willing-ness to face challenges head on, and our child will be so lucky to have you as its mother. I don't de-serve you, I am aware of that, but if you'll forgive me for being such a self-centred jerk, I'll spend the rest of my life trying to. I will do everything in my power to make you love me as much as I love you. This is what I wanted to tell you. All this and how very sorry I am for screwing things up.'

He stopped and put down the mike, the silence deafening, and suddenly all eyes were on her. But she didn't know what to do. She didn't know what to think. Her heart was beating too fast in her chest and her head was spinning so wildly her vision blurred.

But her inner voice of reason, the one that had got her through the many struggles she'd had with her insecurities this past week, was trying to make its way through the chaos. It was insisting that maybe actions spoke louder than words. That maybe he'd been more thrown off balance by her mother's appearance than she'd thought. He was so supremely confident, such a tower of strength, that he appeared invincible. But he wasn't. No one was.

He'd just declared how he felt about her in front of two hundred people. He'd spun the party better than she ever could. He'd addressed her every fear and laid it to rest. All that envy for the baby who had his attention, and her siblings who'd found the happiness she'd never thought she deserved. Well, maybe she did. No. Not maybe. She *did*.

And suddenly, with the last of her defences crumbling to dust, Olympia couldn't stand being so far away from him any longer.

Her heart raced as she set off in his direction, the agog guests parting for her like the sea. He met her halfway and stopped. But she didn't. She walked right up to him, threw her arms around his neck and kissed him with every single thing she could now allow herself to feel for him, oblivious to the whoops and cheers around them.

He held her tight as if he never wanted to let her go, and she could feel the thundering of his heart against her own. 'I've never had anyone fight for me like that before,' she said dizzily when they broke for breath. 'I've never had anyone on my side.'

'I'll never leave it.' His eyes were dark, glazed with passion and emotion, but his expression was grave. 'I'll never stop fighting for you, *agape mou*. I'm so sorry for everything I said. I didn't mean any of it. You were right. I was lashing out. I was terrified. All my adult life I've feared the destruction love can cause. But not anymore. I don't want to be in hock to the past. I intend to make peace with Selene, who you are *nothing* like. It's beyond time. I want to look to the future, a future that includes you and our baby and hopefully many more. Since you came into it, my life has been so much more exciting, so much more everything. I love you. Very much.' He stared into her eyes, and she could see in his a flicker of uncertainty, a vulnerability that indicated his sincerity and intensified the emotion filling her up. 'Do you think in time you might be able to feel the same?'

'No,' she said, smiling up at him, leaning in for another kiss drenched in love. 'Because I already do.'

EPILOGUE

Eleven months later

ON A SATURDAY morning in early June, Olympia stood at the entrance to the Metropolitan Cathedral of Athens and took a moment to survey the achingly beautiful scene before her. The white columns, arches and gilded dome gleamed in the sunlight that streamed in through the windows. Flowers cascaded from urns, and the black and white marble of the floor shone.

Then her gaze landed on Alex. He stood at the other end of the aisle, in front of the altar, so tall, solid and handsome he took her breath away—and everything else simply disappeared.

Leo, his best man and the friend he'd reclaimed.

Elias, their four-month-old son, asleep in the arms of his doting Aunt Daphne.

The guests that filled the pews on both sides, because he'd opened himself up to the idea of friends and was no longer an island.

She could see nothing but him.

They'd come such a long way since the night of the engagement party, she thought, her heart filling with such joy she was surprised it hadn't burst. At work she'd moved into the role she'd wanted and was already outperforming the market. These days she hardly ever had a moment of self-doubt, and she knew her worth because Alex regularly reminded her of it.

As promised, he'd let go of his feelings towards her mother, although he'd made it very clear he'd be taking a zero-tolerance approach. Selene had a front-row seat this morning, and so far had demonstrated exemplary behaviour. Of course, it was still early, and who knew what might happen by nightfall, but she seemed to be just intimidated enough by her soon-to-be son-in-law to toe the line.

The day their son was born had been the happiest of her life. This, everything she'd never dreamed she could have—security, stability, the love of a man she adored—came a very close second.

'Ready?'

In response to Zander's question, Olympia nodded, her throat too thick to speak, because she'd never been readier for anything. The organ struck up, filling the church with music, and she threaded her arm through his. The congregation hushed. Everyone stood and turned. And with a smile that was wide and bright, barely able to contain the happiness swirling around inside her, she walked towards her future.

* * * * *

HARLEQUIN
Reader Service

Enjoyed your book?

Try the perfect subscription for Romance readers and get more great books like this delivered right to your door.

See why over 10+ million readers have tried Harlequin Reader Service.

Start with a Free Welcome Collection with free books and a gift—valued over $20.

Choose any series in print or ebook.
See website for details and order today:

TryReaderService.com/subscriptions